About the Author

Patricia has a medical background having been a practice nurse for many years. She is also a qualified registered healer.
One of her main hobbies is photography and she has had many photographs published in several magazines. Her photographs have been exhibited, with many interpreted and painted at a professional level.
The author was involved with musical theatre for many years taking chorus, cameo and leading roles at the Pier Pavilion in Sussex.
Patricia has won many classes of singing in music festivals.

I Want To Sing Without Crying

This novel is dedicated to my many friends who have
helped and supported me over the years.
I sincerely thank you.

Patricia Rose

I WANT TO SING WITHOUT CRYING

AUSTIN MACAULEY
PUBLISHERS LTD.

Copyright © Patricia Rose

The right of Patricia Rose to be identified as author of this work has been asserted by her in accordance with section 77 and 78 of the Copyright, Designs and Patents Act 1988.

All rights reserved. No part of this publication may be reproduced, stored in a retrieval system, or transmitted in any form or by any means, electronic, mechanical, photocopying, recording, or otherwise, without the prior permission of the publishers.

Any person who commits any unauthorized act in relation to this publication may be liable to criminal prosecution and civil claims for damages.

A CIP catalogue record for this title is available from the British Library.

ISBN 978 184963 385 7

www.austinmacauley.com

First Published (2013)
Austin Macauley Publishers Ltd.
25 Canada Square
Canary Wharf
London
E14 5LB

Printed and Bound in Great Britain

Acknowledgments

To Trevor for his help with the Artistic work; a gem with interpretation.

Chapter One

Sometimes the best laid plans work out but first you have to make them.

Lindy found herself sitting down, a mug of hot soup in her hand, trying to concentrate on her way forward, now that she was beginning another new part of her life.

She propped herself up with two big cushions, and wrapped her hands around the warm mug; comforted by the feeling, she reflected on the almost extraordinary chain of events that had taken her to where she was, right then.

It had been the finalizing of her divorce that had led to the realization that more than her marital status had to change.

Everyone wanted a different part of her and they took, with very little to give back, and she realized that she had been too willing to help which had almost invited people to take advantage, and after much soul searching she concluded that only she could change her life.

Lindy had really taken the bull by the horns and had put her house on the market and made the mammoth decision to leave her stressful nursing position in the neighbouring town. Her job had got too intense, as more and more work was being put her way. She had always been involved and enjoyed working hard but she had begun to feel that she was taken for granted. Just the journey to work was fraught with frustration, through what seemed to be permanent road works and diversions. It was a daily challenge, before she even started her work, and something she could no longer find the energy or dedication to continue. It was definitely something she could do without.

She shifted her body on the sofa and brushed her hands through her red hair as she recalled the situation, and let out a long sigh, to release the tension.

Suddenly, after some time, her house had sold quickly and the new owners had requested that there be only a short time before they moved in. So the big decision to leave work was made, much to many people's amazement.

With the help, encouragement and support from her long term friend Tony, she had moved away from the familiar area, to one she hardly knew at all, as she had been drawn to the wonderful countryside of Yorkshire.

Tony's work had taken Lindy into the North, when he had invited her to accompany him on the long, boring journey. She had readily agreed, as she confessed she was intrigued to know more about the countryside north of the Watford Gap.

A faint smile flickered across her face when she thought about Robert; an artist she had discovered completely by chance, a few months earlier.

They had gradually built up a strong friendship, through phone calls and emails but it was far from smooth. The distance between them accentuated it, and now her life changing decision had brought them strategically closer together. She knew she had to make her own way in her newly chosen environment, and although she was looking forward to making a new life, Lindy was very much aware it would be far from easy. At least she had learnt, although only a few hundred miles away, she was going into a very different culture and language, and was well aware that she had to learn fast.

She had moved away from her family and friends to start a new life and it was almost as if she had been psychologically kicked away from the mundane, predictable routine she was almost sucked into.

It all stemmed from a completely simple and innocent thought that had led to such a life changing situation for her. She realised she had almost no control on that, as she felt deep, deep down, she was going in the right direction with her life. Although there was no goal to aim for, she would find one.

After much hard work trawling through local information, and investigations she had met many interesting and kind people. Thanks to email, she still had regular contact with the 'old' friends she had left behind.

As she thought about the artist, Robert, she felt a warm glow slowly wash over her and was conscious of the amazing connection they had and how so often when he called her, sometimes late at night, they said the same thing at the same time. Similarly, she realised how volatile and unpredictable he could be, and she became increasingly wary, which deeply saddened her. The up-side of his personality was his passion, and the emotion he showed was breathtaking. It certainly was not for the faint hearted; when he showed his feelings it was all consuming, almost in contrast to his gentle, almost innocent child like outward persona. It was wonderful when they were together.

Lindy got up from the sofa, put the empty mug into the sink, checked her appearance in the small kitchen mirror, grabbed her handbag and coat, took the keys for the car from the hall table and drove in to town. There were a few things she needed from the supermarket as her fridge was unusually almost empty.

She parked the car and searched around for the list of items she needed; feeling in all her pockets and almost tipping out the complete contents of her handbag; Nothing. It must still be on the kitchen table. Feeling very cross with herself, and not inclined to drive back home she entered the store, found a big trolley, as there were no small ones to be seen and started to systematically walk along the aisles one by one, trying to remember what she needed.

Satisfied that she had all the important items, she took her purse from her handbag and paid at the check-out. She put the items back into the trolley and began to wheel it to the car, when suddenly a woman approached her and with a commanding voice told her,

"Stop right there!"

Lindy was so shocked at this outburst she stopped immediately. The woman was shorter than her with short black hair cut in a severe style. She was quite rotund, but all Lindy could see was her tight lips moving, and her arms put up to prevent her from walking forward and pointing in her direction as she announced that she was a store detective. Unable to speak, Lindy heard the woman accuse her of taking goods that had not been paid for, and insisted that she turn around, at the same time grabbing her arm tightly, saying she was taking her straight to the manager's office.

In shock and still unable to say a word and still clutching the handle of the trolley she was marched along the side of the store, in full view of many shoppers who were glaring at her. She had no idea where she was going, but eventually the tight grip on her arm eased as she was almost pushed into a small long room, where a thin man was sitting.

The door was slammed shut behind them as she was confronted by the thin man who stood up and informed her that he was the manager of the store.

She was then instructed to sit down as the woman proceeded to tell the manager that she had found a shoplifter, who had taken items without paying.

Lindy started to speak, but was told, in no uncertain terms, to keep quiet until she was spoken to. The detective asked for the till roll and itemised products, and proceeded to go through her trolley item by item. The manager checked the list, as they took everything out and placed in on a side table, until there was only her handbag left. That too was removed, but underneath, there was a bag of sliced ham. This was not on the till roll.

Lindy stared in disbelief and immediately offered to pay for it. The manager and the store detective glanced at each other, without saying anything. Lindy's overwhelming need to get out was beginning to tell. She insisted that she had not bought the ham, and repeated that she would pay for it, but her words fell on deaf ears. The manager sat down, reached for the telephone and called the police.

She began to feel very sick as the realization of her predicament became very clear as they all sat in silence; until the knock came on the door. The manager opened it to two policemen in uniform. They were quickly told that they had a shoplifter and that the store was going to prosecute. They nodded, and taking the trolley with the items she had paid for, leaving the ham, she was escorted to her car. The policemen watched as Lindy unloaded her shopping into the boot of her car, and having put the trolley away she was told to drive straight to the police station, and that an officer would sit beside her, and stressed she should follow his colleague and he would be watching her every move.

At this stage Lindy began to shiver, as she explained that she did not know where the police station was, as she had only recently moved into the area. It seemed that the look on her face told him it was true, and repeated that she follow the police car in front of her. Almost unable to put the car key in to the lock, she managed to start the engine. With her whole body shaking, she drove behind the police car to the station. The officer quickly got out of the car and using hand signals, directed to where she should park.

They entered the police station where a desk clerk was told that they had a shoplifter, and asked which interview room was available. Taking hold of her arm, she was almost pulled along the narrow corridor. The grip became even stronger as they stopped outside a door. The policeman opened it and calmly asked Lindy to sit down on a chair, at the side of a long table. In her confusion, she did exactly as she was asked. He then said he would return with his colleague, so that they could take down her statement of events and left her alone in the stark room. Pulling her coat closely around her, she huddled herself, perching on the edge of the chair. In her now muddled and confused mind she thought that the two policemen would soon come through the door. She had no idea of the time, so glanced at her wrist watch. She had left home over an hour ago.

It was quite a long time before the door of the interview room opened and the two policemen entered, and silently sat down on two chairs opposite Lindy.

Not knowing what was going to happen next, she just lowered her head, to avoid their penetrating gaze. Then the policeman who had taken her to the room began to speak.

"I am going to ask you questions, and my colleague will write down your answers. Is that clear? We want to know your recollection of the events that occurred earlier today"

Lindy just nodded barely raising her head to look at him.

She was asked her full name, address and age, and her telephone number. She managed to control her voice as she answered. Then the serious questions began.

Why had she gone shopping? Where was her list? Why did she buy the ham and why did she conceal it. The same questions in various forms were asked over and over again. Each time, without any hesitation, Lindy told them she had not bought any ham; especially as she was a vegetarian. With a slight, almost nervous, shift of his body it was then suggested that she had bought it for someone else. Struggling to keep calm, she repeated that she had not bought any ham.

Finally the questions stopped, and she was presented with the paper on which the officer had been writing, and was told to sign it. She read it through as carefully as she could, but the words kept blending into one another, as the strain was taking its toll on her. She was innocent, but was being treated as if she were guilty, and that anger alone made her furious, almost beyond belief. She began to tell them again that she had done nothing wrong, but the officer who had asked most of the questions, just put his hand up, as he said to her.

"I have had enough of hearing from you, just follow me." Without another word he turned, opened the door and walked down the corridor. Lindy obeyed. She had no other choice, as she was escorted out of the interview room, and back into the main reception area she was asked if she needed a solicitor. Immediately she replied,

"It is not necessary as I have done nothing wrong."

She wanted to say more, but could see that the attention span of the officer had gone as he asked for all her personal effects to be taken from her, and logged in a book. Again she was asked to sign that it was correct. They were placed in a rudimentary hessian bag and the cord secured. She then had her finger prints taken. The officer took her shaking hand and plunged it into an ink pad, then with a tight grip, rolled each one from side to side, making its mark in the correct indicated slot on the paper. She was offered a small piece of cloth to wipe the dye off, but it was barely adequate as it was swiftly taken away and then a policewoman told her to follow her into a room, further down the hall. Feeling very sick and light-headed Lindy obeyed as her strength was fast draining away as she tried to control herself and not give in to the almost overwhelming need to shout out her innocence. With a clank of the key opening the iron door she was put into a holding cell. Without a word the policewoman left and the door was slammed with a reverberating noise behind her.

Lindy began to shake all over as she tried to grasp what on earth was happening. She managed to look around, although there was not much to see. The cell had no outside light at all, only a single dull light from the centre of the ceiling. There was a small bench and a seatless toilet in the corner; otherwise the room was dark and bare.

She looked at the toilet and suddenly realized her bladder was full and she needed to go to the loo right then. There had been so much going on she had not realized how badly she needed to relieve herself and tugging at her clothes, she only just made it in time. The urine just gushed out of her as she sat on the cold ceramic bowl. She was there long after she had let everything out, and looked around for a toilet roll but there was not one to be seen. Feeling unclean, she searched in her pocket, and found a crumpled tissue, and used that to wipe herself. It was not adequate but certainly better than nothing. At least they had not taken that away from her in fear of what she might do; goodness only knows what they assumed. She pulled up her knickers, straightened her clothes, and searched for a handle to flush but there was not one. She glared down at her excrement as it lay at the bottom of the bowl before she went back to sit down on the cold bench, and wait.

As her watch had been taken from her, she had absolutely no idea of the time and was increasingly aware she needed to be back at home to receive a call from her daughter, who had just been on a trial session before starting her new Saturday job, and they had arranged to speak later that day.

Lindy sat huddled upon the wooden bench and strained her ears for any sign that would give her hope that she would soon be out of the cell, but the only sound was of the occasional muffled voices, but she could not decipher what they were saying and the intonation was not of any help either. She continued to sit and wait, still shivering and holding her stomach which was in knots as the tears rolled down her face, but she made no noise.

Suddenly a key turned in her cell door, and the policewoman entered. With no emotion in her face or voice, she told Lindy to follow her down the corridor. Again she was asked if she needed a solicitor but, by this time, all she could do was to shake her head and whimper.

"I have done nothing wrong."

Her personal effects were carelessly poured out of the hessian sack onto the top of the reception table with an intermittent thud. She was asked to check it was all correct and sign that she had received all her possessions. Barely able to hold the pen, she signed, hardly recognising her own signature.

Lindy had to ask where the exit from the police station was, as her eyes, although fully open, were unable to take in her environment. She managed to find her car, open the door and somehow drove home.

She parked in her driveway, took out her shopping and almost threw it on the floor of the kitchen in disgust and frustration and as she did so, she saw the shopping list she had left behind. In desperation she carefully checked it, and of course, there was no ham on the list. Why should there be?

Although she had been out longer than she had expected she looked at the phone and knew it had not rung. Trusting her instincts she poured herself a glass of water and as she gulped at it to try and stop her body shaking the house phone rang. Taking a deep breath and composing herself as much as possible Lindy answered it. It was her daughter as arranged. She did not need to say anything other than,

"Hello."

Colleen was so excited and happy as she told her how her first day had been and her enthusiasm just flew out as Lindy listened intently to what she was describing. She was so glad that Colleen was happy, and after congratulating her as cheerily as should could, they said goodbye and she put down the phone.

There was no way in the world she could tell her daughter what had happened in her day.

Chapter Two

A couple of months had quickly passed by, and Lindy had found out so much more about the beautiful countryside she was living in.

She had been on a couple of short art courses with the intention to understand and learn about water colour and oil painting, as it had been several years since she had 'taken up the brush' and she was not at all surprised that unfortunately most of her attempted work was a disaster. But the upside was good as she had met some fascinating characters and two interesting and talented women who only attended the short courses, to 'keep their hand in.' One lady, who she got on very well with, had invited her to her beautiful home that was, as she described it, just above the snow line. On a clear day it overlooked the valley and in to the far distance beyond and almost to the sea.

Lindy attended the courses as she really wanted to recall her past tuition and to try to understand the work that Robert did for his living. She could have easily asked him, but she felt the need to find out by herself and not even tell him, well not at first anyway. The results that she came home with were bordering on embarrassing, and she knew it would be quite a while before she plucked up the courage to show him, and hoped he would be able to laugh; apart from setting fire to them it was probably the only other option!

She knew he was totally dedicated to his work which was very time consuming, so there were times when they did not meet up, if he was absorbed in the current canvas. It was times like this when he became very out of touch with reality and when they spoke on the phone he was frequently short tempered, perhaps bordering on aggressive. He had shown signs of this side of his personality often and it was a side of him that deeply upset her, as she tried to excuse him and put it down to pressure of work, and deadlines. His other softer side was so inviting and he was often very funny too, and they frequently dissolved into uncontrollable giggles, which ultimately led to his passionate nature taking over, which she found increasingly intriguing.

Since her life changing move, her artist friend Robert was elusive at times, and she was tempted to call him 'The Pimpernel' but that was only a thought she had and never let him know. But at one point in complete frustration, she had picked up the phone to call him. Her call rang out and his familiar voice answered.

She just gently said "Hello."

There was silence, then she heard him crash down his handset.

She could almost feel and taste his desire and fear all rolled into one, but with immediate irritation she said to herself.

"Right! Now I know where I stand; there is not much doubt about that."

Her next internet connection was about to be installed as there had been several bad providers, but this time she was hopeful that her final decision was a good one and until then there was nothing she could do. His rudeness had rather taken her by surprise and she began to feel cross with him and herself, as she should have known better from having several times in the past been on the receiving end of his irrational emotional behaviour.

Although feeling very disappointed she was still going to ask him to paint another image for her; something she had thought about on and off for a very long time and somehow felt it was only Robert who would paint it right for her. She had met several good artists during her summer courses, but still it was Robert she wanted to ask and because of their intimate relationship, she knew he could feel and connect with her thoughts and feelings in a second. She did seriously challenge her motives when she decided to ask Robert, after all he was still married, but she had dismissed them as almost trivial after what he had said to her; although Lindy had to admit that it was his emotional passion that made her decision almost out of her earthly control but she knew he would get it right.

Late September was warm and mostly sunny. After a busy wiggly - wobbly, interesting but exhausting summer, Lindy decided that she wanted a short holiday before the colder, darker days set in, and told Robert she was going away for a few days. When he heard this he invited her to see him before she left.

They had met up at his invitation for just for a short time at his studio, and it was very obvious almost as soon as she knocked on his office door that he was very pleased to see her. As he opened the door he took her in his arms and hugged her as she felt his racing heart beat against her breast. His mouth searched for hers as they were locked in an embrace, that went on and on until he gently moved his lips away to say,

"Lindy I want you right now."

At the same time he was tugging at her skirt, pulled down her panties and carefully sitting her down on his very large chair, felt for her and pulled her hands to feel his hard erection. He entered her and with only a few movements was crying out with pleasure at his sexual release.

He lay relaxed on the floor for a few minutes before looking up and smiling at her and softly saying,

"Thank you, now I can get on with my work."

"What do you mean?" she asked, not quite understanding, and feeling slightly confused by his action.

It was obvious that Robert wanted to explain to her, but she could see him momentarily hang back before he said in his straightforward way.

"That is how men are programmed, just like an egg timer, the brain is good but thoughts and feelings slowly drain like fine grains of sand almost undetected to your balls. As they build almost to bursting point and are finally released, it clears your brain, so you can really concentrate on your work and that it exactly how it is with me."

He watched her face intently as he spoke to her.

"You can go now and I am very grateful for your understanding. Have a good break, I'll miss you."

He got up from the floor and gently kissed her, but with a definite unspoken dismissal he walked to politely open his studio door to let her out.

Lindy left Robert to compose himself and she drove home, her mind in a complete whirl as to what had just happened and wondered what was to happen in the future. She slowly began to feel increasingly irritated by the way she almost allowed him to treat her, but made excuses to herself that she had been caught off guard and that he was a gentle man and he had tried to explain to her how he felt, the best way he knew how.

She had looked in the newspapers and flicked through several brochures until she was drawn to an advertisement of a hotel not very far away, with a spa wing attached. It did not take very long before making up her mind to make a reservation for a few days. The thought of having everything done for her was very appealing as it would give her time to relax and carefully plan ahead. When she told her new friends of her idea, they all asked to go with her, which Lindy really appreciated, but this time she felt the need to go alone. Jokingly they had said they would forgive her, just the once.

It was a glorious day when she drove to the hotel, a journey which had taken just over an hour, as she did not feel the need to push her highly powered car to the limit. She was grateful for the installed satnav system as it was very useful and made her journey into another unknown area so much easier.

The hotel came into sight and Lindy approached the entrance through two high wide pillars with a regal lion proudly lying on top of each one. The strong iron gates stood open which led down a straight road lined on each side with magnificent high trees. It was a beautiful sight, as the autumn leaves were just beginning to turn colour.

As she approached the grounds it was difficult to ignore the enormous signs that told anyone entering that there was a ten mile an hour speed restriction. She immediately looked at her speedometer and applied the brakes, as she drove down the road that led into a semi-circle leading to the grand front doors. She stopped to drop off her case, and parked in a vacant space nearby. Collecting her suitcase she wheeled it in to the reception area to her right. She noticed on the other side were a couple of welcoming armchairs, and a sofa beside a gas fire which was flickering flames in an enormous ornate black fireplace.

Lindy checked herself in, and was handed her key and room number from the charming good looking young lady receptionist. As she turned around, almost out of nowhere, came a young man in uniform who asked if he could assist her with her luggage to her room. She was grateful, and was glad she did not have to find her own way. This done, she thanked him, gave him a small tip, and he left.

Her room was not very big but it certainly had wonderful views of the small lake in the grounds. She made some tea from the hospitality tray, sipping it and munched on a ginger biscuit as she started to unpack. Perhaps because of the journey, or the fact that she was going to be waited on, or just everything that had happened, she began to feel very tired so, closing the thick curtains, and partly undressing she slid under the duvet for a short nap and feeling warm and comfortable, she relaxed and began to doze.

How long after she had got into bed was uncertain when the sound of a key turning in the lock made her wake up, and as she became more aware, her ears were on alert, but there was no sound. Still she sensed there was someone in her room as she listened carefully not daring to move. Then there was a sound of soft footsteps approaching her bed. Trying to listen she lay completely still, hardly baring to even breathe. Then she felt a hand on her legs and a quiet voice of a man saying he wanted to get to know her, at the same time reaching under the duvet and sliding his hands up her thighs and all but reaching her crotch as his breathing began to get louder and faster.

Immediately Lindy was completely aware of what was happening and shouted out to him to get out and leave her alone but he continued trying to touch her with his violating hands as he attempted to stroke and rub her.

Lindy became so angry she began to scream at the top of her voice to get him out of her room. She just kept on screaming,

"Get out. Get out!"

The attempted fondling stopped and in a second her bedroom door slammed closed. She flopped back onto her bed exhausted. What on earth had happened? She felt dirty, so slightly opening the curtains to let some daylight in, she pushed a chair under the door handle and took a long relaxing shower, as she tried to get to grips with what she had just been through.

Her mind whirled round and round. Would she be able to pick him out when she went downstairs? Her room had been very dark, as the curtains were fitted with a black-out lining. He had only said a few words, and in her trauma she was not confident that she could identify him like that either. This was not a good beginning to a relaxing holiday. Drawing on her inner strength she decided that in spite of the bad start she would enjoy herself. Feeling calmer now, Lindy made some more tea and ate a banana. She was not looking forward to going downstairs to look around, or to have the evening meal. She knew that, for at least the time being, she could not report the ghastly incident to anyone as she was sure that no-one would believe her. Thankfully Lindy was alright but felt very much on her guard. The chair was still under the door handle, as she began to unpack her suitcase and hang all her clothes up in the wardrobe.

Lindy put on some casual loose clothes, and with fierce determination took the chair away from the door and made her way downstairs. This time using the lift. She started to investigate and found several different rooms. One for games such as table tennis and snooker and bar billiards, then another 'silent' room, where residents could read books or write letters and another for general sitting and chatting. There were also a couple of coffee shops and a restaurant .

Lindy noticed that almost at the end of the main corridor was a large bowl of apples and oranges with a notice to 'Help yourself'. She looked at a very big juicy orange and took one. Further along was a notice board showing the extra spa options available. Feeling drawn to this she read the details very carefully; she had a list sent through the post but she had not booked any sessions. There were only a few slots available during the time she was there and quickly deciding the most relaxing treatment would be a body massage for the following morning and went to the main reception area to book it. The young lady opened up her screen account and added it on, and advised her to attend wearing her underwear and a towelling dressing gown that was provided in her room.

Feeling more relaxed now, she walked back down the corridors and looked around the shop that sold all the products that were used in the hotel, and many more inviting things to tempt the guests.

As she entered the dining room she was greeted by a smiling face of a young waitress who invited her to sit where ever she liked. There were several young waiters too, but she tried not to catch their eye. There were quite a few tables, all set out for a different number of people. As she was quite early she chose a table for four right up against the window that looked out onto a lawn with a lit statue and a fountain of water flowing out. It was soothing to watch in the twilight of the day.

Shortly after sitting down, she was joined by a fairly elderly lady, who introduced herself as Ethel. They exchanged pleasantries as their orders were taken. While they waited, Ethel said she had been to the hotel several times before, and found it very welcoming, and had met many interesting people on her visits over the years. She was a widow and the stimulating company gave her many hours of pleasure once she returned to her home, where she now lived, alone.

Lindy was very interested in all Ethel had to say, as the next two courses were served. They drank wine and had a giggle. Lindy decided not to tell Ethel what had happened to her earlier in the day. She did not want to spoil her euphoria. It was all behind her now.

When it was completely dark outside they agreed that they were both tired and saying a warm goodnight, they made their way to the lift. She was only too glad to open her room door, and carefully placing the chair under the door handle, she quickly showered again, got into bed and was soon in a deep sleep.

Another sunny day greeted Lindy as she drew back her curtains. The undisturbed rest had done her good and in spite of yesterday, she felt glad that she had taken a short holiday. Just to have meals made was relaxing.

She had not made any direct plans to meet Ethel and was glad not to be tied to anytime. As she entered the dining room for a buffet style breakfast, she could not help but scan the tables to see if she was there. She could not see her, so made her way to a table with her selected plates of food. She began to tuck into the delicious fruit salad, when suddenly Ethel appeared carrying her food on a tray.

When they had eaten all they could Ethel suggested a stroll in the grounds, to show Lindy around. It was so good to have a kind person as her guide, as Ethel explained that she was keen to show Lindy something. They rounded a corner and there was an enormous spreading mulberry tree and not far away they could hear a babbling brook. As they got closer Lindy could see that after many years the water had cut a deep channel in the earth and stood to listen to the sound and watched the clear water as it sparkled in its fast flow, only to disappear underground. The air was clean and crisp, and the heavy dew glistened under their feet and their prints left a tell-tale trail in the lush grass.

They walked very slowly side by side, taking in the beauty of the surroundings in early autumn. Then suddenly Lindy asked Ethel what time it was, as unusually she had not put her watch on, and neither had her friend. Making an apologetic retreat she ran back to the hotel and found she only had a short time before her massage. Quickly taking the lift, she went back to her room, put on the recommended attire and went to the spa reception area. This time there was a young lady on reception who registered her arrival, and invited her to sit while she waited for her therapist to collect her. Therapist sounded a bit heavy, but she did as she was told and sat down and watched the fish in a large tank as they played; it was very soothing.

After a few minutes her name was called and she looked up to see a smiling young man all dressed in white, who introduced himself as Leo, her therapist. Lindy felt slightly surprised, although she had received massages from men before. Their natural stronger upper body was a bonus to their work if the client liked a firm massage but it was usually after being asked. Surprisingly this time they had not asked. She followed him to his room. He politely confirmed she was there for a basic body massage, and showed her into a tiny area, and pulled the curtains closed. He asked her to take off all her clothes and put on the dressing gown provided and minute paper pants.

Pulling the dressing gown tightly around her she emerged from the changing area and was ushered in to the treatment area which was beautifully set out, with gentle soothing music playing in the background. The young man repeated that his name was Leo as he gave her a large warm, deep soft towel to place over her, as he took the dressing gown from her. He asked her to lie face down on the couch and she found the small hole for her face to pop through for her comfort. He then went to the top of the bed and with a soft voice said it could be cold for just a moment as he dropped the massage oil onto her back. The music was very spiritual and almost hypnotic as she began to relax. But as he started, his strong rhythmic movements were uncomfortable and she felt every muscle tense as her senses became alert. His massage continued and she began to relax as it became very soothing, not too strong but a definite pressure. Having massaged her back and shoulders he moved the towel to cover her back and began to massage her buttocks and legs; He was very good at his job.

Just as she had almost fallen asleep, Leo asked her to turn over, as he deftly placed the towel over her breasts and abdomen, and pouring a few more drops of cold essence on her he began to massage her shoulders and arms. He then asked if she wanted her stomach to be massaged, and immediately Lindy replied,

"No. Thank you."

Without saying another word he went straight to the end of the treatment bed and began to work on her legs. His strokes were firm and confident, but, as he raised her legs, one by one, she began to wonder what he was thinking. Having had her eyes closed for most of the time, she opened them and carefully watched his face. Perhaps realizing that he was being watched Leo continued to massage her legs. At this point trying not to assume anything she just thought to herself.

'My, I am glad I had a leg wax last week!'

Shortly afterwards he said he had almost finished. Feeling relaxed and tingling she pulled the towel up over herself as much as it would allow, and then as he left the bottom of the bed his fingers still in contact with her, he ran his hand up her thigh and went straight to her crotch, and with heavy breathing he attempted to massage her.

She started to push him away and began to scream and jumped off the couch, grabbing the towel to cover what was left of her dignity, and ran to get her clothes. As she did so she caught a glimpse of him by the side of the pool, his trouser bulging, just before dramatically plunging into it making a big splash in his wake. There was little doubt in her mind what his intention was and as fast as she could, she put on the essential clothes and managed to run back to hotel reception area. Feeling safer she flopped into one of the comfy chairs and thought long and hard as fortunately the reception was empty so she had time gather her thoughts. What would she say? Who would she say it to? The most important fact was, how could she prove it? How could she prove any of it? At least he had not done any real damage; but it was obvious what he had in mind, or perhaps it was expected of him. No! Surely not? That thought was ridiculous and at the same time her body began to shake so she made her way back to her room. Putting the chair up against the door, she fell on the bed and sobbed her heart out. She cried until there was nothing left and as she lay on her bed she knew she had to do something, but what? Just then she was not certain as she lay and thought as her breathing gradually returned to normal.

One thing Lindy concluded was that she had to leave the hotel as she could not prove anything that had happened to her, and as a result felt very angry and depressed. Fighting her desire to leave immediately she tried to be practical, so she went in to lunch and was fortunate to find Ethel, and was able to distract her thoughts and ask her what she had done that morning after their walk. All Lindy wanted was someone to take away her pain, and lovely Ethel with her soft and gentle way was just right, as she began to tell Lindy another story in her long and interesting life.

Grateful that she had found Ethel, she listened intently to her reminiscence and watched her eyes as she spoke.

They were served lunch, but Lindy found she could not eat very much and only picked at the delicious meal in front of her. Realizing something was wrong, Ethel asked why she was not eating, staring right back in to her eyes. Taken unawares Lindy explained that there was trouble at home and needed to leave. She looked at Ethel and somehow knew she did not believe her, but she was lady enough not to ask anymore.

Lindy got up from her seat and hugged her dear friend until she could hardly breathe. They had exchanged addresses and telephone numbers and Lindy promised to keep in touch; the hug was long and meaningful and as she released her grip she almost ran out of the dining room.

She packed up her suitcase and went to the reception and explained she had to leave early due to family problems. Fortunately they were very kind and understanding as she knew she could not handle anymore opposition at that time. She paid her bill, and although a young man offered to take her suitcase to her car she politely refused and through gritted teeth said she was quite capable of pulling it along on its wheels to her car. The day had become overcast and dull and a few spots of rain fell on the windscreen as she began her journey home.

While she was driving, she could not help but go over the extraordinary events that had happened to her on her 'holiday' and felt disgusted and confused about the two men who had tried to violate her. Even in the worst case scenario, she had in no way given them the wrong signals and of that she was sure. In spite of them she thought of Ethel and what a lovely lady she was, and felt a warmth towards her, because if she hadn't been there for her, she would have seen things from a different perspective altogether. Ethel had helped to keep her dignity, under extremely difficult circumstances.

. Lindy was so relieved to arrive back home. The holiday to recharge her internal batteries had been far from the refuge she so badly needed and she had certainly seen life at its best and the most degrading, all under one roof. There was nothing she could do to get retribution for what she had been through as she knew she had no proof of anyone being unprofessional, and that really made her seriously angry.

She unpacked her suitcase and put her clothes into the washing machine as she needed to get the hotel out of her system, and this was one way of doing it.

Feeling a bit peckish now, she defrosted a large brown roll and opened a can of soup. When it was ready she enjoyed every mouthful. When she had finished she just put her used crockery by the side of the sink. She had a long hot bath with lavender essences and fell in to her own bed, knowing she did not have to put a chair up against her bedroom door handle.

It was only a few weeks later that a letter came through her letter box. It was from Ethel's daughter informing her that Ethel had died shortly after their visit to the hotel and she wanted Lindy to know how much her Mother had appreciated her friendship; so much so, that she had left her a small gift. It would be in the post very soon.

Feeling overwhelmed as she thought of her kind friend, she decided to call her daughter and give her condolences in person. Luckily her daughter was in and sounded very glad that Lindy had rung, but understandably sounded very sad. Lindy wanted to ask her many questions but she sensed it would be inappropriate, and reluctantly, she thanked her and put down the phone.

When the parcel arrived Lindy opened her present, and found a delicate solid silver filigree of a centre of a watch. It could be used as a necklace as it had an attachment on the top.

Just like Ethel she thought; delicate, hard working, and reliable. Quiet but strong.

Remembering her friend and how much she had helped her through a very difficult time, unbeknown to her. Or perhaps, she did have an unexplained inner knowledge, which, if Lindy was truthful, she should and could have picked up. She had been all consumed with what had happened. She had not been strong enough to stand back and see the situation as it really was.

Overtaken by self pity, she put her head in her hands and cried. But somehow the tears did not come, as momentarily she saw Ethel in her mind's eye and knew she would not have approved.

Feeling foolish, as if someone was watching her, she sat up and admired her gift She knew that silver is stronger than gold, as she had learnt a few years back in her psychic development group; gold was feminine and silver was masculine. The sun is feminine and the moon is masculine. Dear Ethel had a deeper understanding than she had realized. She had sent strength to her, and Lindy knew she had to take up the challenge. It would be one way of thanking Ethel for her trust and be the person she knew she could be. Somehow, along the way, she had lost her way, but looking outward and being positive was the way forward. She remembered someone saying to her a long time ago.

'You are never given more than you can achieve.'

Right, she thought, that does it for me! Watch out world here I come!

Chapter Three

The thought of Robert crossed her mind from time to time, but his refusal to speak to her on the phone in the past hung heavily on her mind.

He had said he was unhappy in his long, loveless marriage, and had told her that he would leave. They had not discussed how he planned to do it, or for that matter, when.

Lindy still wanted him to paint a picture for her. She had bought a painting of a moody, atmospheric country scene at dusk, many years before, and she was fond of it, but something was missing, and felt confident that Robert could sort it out and make sensible and artistic suggestions.

The picture was obviously of an early autumnal evening, as there were only a few leaves left on the trees. The scene outside her window was very similar and it spurred her onto try and contact Robert again. This time she would not telephone, but send an email instead, explaining her idea and asking him to help her, at the same thinking very carefully as to how to word her request, as his artistic temperament was so easily upset. She'd learnt that soon after they became friends. Knowing he had never seen the picture, she would ask him if he would visit, but only if he would consider the work and talk to her about his professional feelings. Giving him an outline of the painting, she read and re-read the email before finally, taking a deep breath, sent it. Gone!

As she sat back in her chair, she hoped the 'gods' were smiling at that time; then mentally scolded herself. How totally ridiculous, all this fuss, just because she wanted a picture. But, that was how it was. He could be so volatile, she had to be careful, as his reactions at times almost sent her spinning. Then her sense of humour clicked in and she could visualise him wearing a t-shirt with the logo:

' Approach at your peril'.

They were always so close and happy when they were together, as the atmosphere became very highly charged with art and ideas and when they touched it was genuinely beautiful.

In spite of everything that was good, Lindy was not confident that he would reply at all, and certainly not straight away; so she got up and went to the under stairs cupboard, got out the iron and ironing board. She had been putting it off for too long and the pile was getting quite high, which, in itself put her off straight away. It was not one of her favourite household chores so she turned on the radio and listened to some music to help her through the mundane task.

Just as she had almost finished her telephone rang; she walked over to answer it, wondering if it was Robert. It was a client of hers who wanted to discuss a difficult situation and to have a short session of healing. They arranged a mutual convenient time the following day.

She finished the ironing, folded the board away and took the clothes upstairs, put them on hangers and went down to the computer room. What a surprise; Robert had replied to her. She opened his email and read that he was quite interested in her idea and would like to see it first, before making a decision. He went on to make a couple of suggestions as to when he could visit her. They agreed in a couple of day's time, as she told him she had a client the next day. It would be around mid-morning, and he added that should there be any problems then he would telephone her.

The next two days ended up much busier that Lindy had expected, but she was quite pleased as she had seen another client who had been recommended to her. He was a pleasant middle aged man with almost no self confidence. He was worried that he may lose his job, as younger men appeared to have so much going for them. It had been a very interesting consultation. As he paid her, he smiled, just a little bit and said how much he had enjoyed the session. He still could not hold her gaze for more than a second. Lindy offered him her business card and invited him to call her if he needed her help again.

The morning dawned on the day that Robert was to visit. The weather was dull and overcast, which was a bit disappointing, but it did not stop her heart 'flipping' from time to time in her anticipation of seeing him again.

She remembered the wonderful day when he had said how much he cared for her, and that he was in the wrong relationship. He had hugged and kissed her until her lips were almost numb. Then he almost disappeared into oblivion and left her in an emotional turmoil. She had uncovered a gentle caring, and loving man, with deep emotions he kept seriously suppressed. Early in their relationship she had felt confident enough to actually light heartedly accuse him of 'emotional anorexia'.

Lindy glanced at the bedside clock, 'Oops', just enough time to shower, dress and have some breakfast without rushing too much. Flying around like a woman possessed would help nothing and no-one. She felt so silly when she had a moment of reflection as to how she was feeling and reacting. Her teenage years were long gone, but she was behaving just like one and being conscious of her thoughts and feeling did nothing to help her.

She had already decided what to wear. She stepped into a plain three quarter length black skirt with buttons all down the front. It clung nicely over her feminine hips, and was comfortable too. She left the last two buttons undone, to allow for a bit of movement, and complimented it by a top in a plain deep pink with a white collar. The colour emphasised her thick red hair which she had recently had cut into an elfin like shape, which highlighted her high cheek bones; adding just a touch of makeup she stepped into a pair of black high heeled shoes. It was almost inappropriate, but as Robert was so much taller, it made talking easier if they were standing up; and if she wanted to hug him; and she knew she wanted to hug him so much and to feel his warm arms wrapped around her.

Lindy put on a CD of relaxing music that she knew he liked, sat down and closed her eyes as she took in a deep breath. As she exhaled she started to giggle out loud. If anyone could see her now they too would roar with laughter at her stupidity. After all, Robert was only a man, and they weren't going out anywhere either! She fought with herself that it was only respectful to try and look nice if you were expecting a guest. Well she decided, he wasn't even that really. The battle in her mind went on as she tried to concentrate on the calming music which at that moment wasn't working too well.

Her door bell chimed, she opened her eyes and taking another deep breath she got up from the chair, and almost immediately all but fell over, as one of her heels got caught in the rug. Steadying herself she walked to the door, and opened it to a smiling Robert. She invited him in, took his coat and hung it on the rack in the hall and pretending not to notice his outstretched arms, she asked if he would like some coffee as she turned away to go into the kitchen. His voice, very close behind her said,

"That would be very nice."

She had already put the coffee machine on and the aroma was delicious as it wafted around the room.

Cups in hand, Robert with his coffee and Lindy with her lemonade, made their way to the sitting room, which was much more comfortable. She had long ago explained to him that having had a major operation she was unable to drink coffee or eat many other foods either, as doing so would have a very bad effect on her. He had been polite, but she was sure that he did not understand. Not many people did.

The music was still playing softly in the background and as he sat down he remarked on how calming it was, and visibly began to relax on the other end of the sofa. They chatted lightly about this and that, as Lindy fought hard to prevent herself asking him why he had put the phone down on her as it was now registering high on her 'need to know' list.

After a while, Robert asked to see the painting that she wanted his opinion on. Stupidly, she had forgotten to put it in the sitting room for him to contemplate. How could she have forgotten to get it out for him to look at? How could she have forgotten the reason he was there? Well, she thought, making excuses for herself in her head, after all the time that had gone by there could be no sensible reason other than her confusion with their love affair, as he had obviously changed his mind about his, so called unhappy marriage, that he had spent so much time convincing her of.

Dismissing the intruding thoughts she almost jumped up, but having high heeled shoes on she slowly got to her feet, and at the same time explaining that it was in the back bedroom, and she would bring it down to him. Robert was immediately beside her and insisted that he go to the picture, then she would have no need to bring it down. Slightly taken aback, and feeling a bit silly, she smiled and agreed it was the most sensible thing to do; although it was not heavy it was the practical option considering her lack of organisation, which was way out of character.

They climbed the stairs; Lindy lead the way sensing Robert very close behind her, when suddenly he gave a cheeky pat on her bottom. Trying to ignore it and without turning round she only said,

"Stop it and behave."

He did not reply as they reached the top of the staircase. The door to the second bedroom was open and there, straight in front of them was the painting he had come to see. The dull day outside seemed to almost add an extra atmosphere to the canvas.

Lindy stood aside as Robert entered the room. He stood a distance from it as he looked at it straight on and she watched his face as he slowly scanned the picture. It was quite a while before he said anything and then he was direct with his opinion, as most Northern born people are. He certainly liked the idea and commented that the basic composition was very good and the scene and autumnal colours appealed to him, and agreed that there was certainly something missing He continued to take in the details of the picture for a further few minutes, before turning to Lindy, who was still looking at his face. He suggested that he would think about it and would contact her with his ideas.

That done, she turned to leave the room, but Robert touched her arm, at the same time pulling her towards him. Within a second, the old feelings for him began to rise in her until it was almost overwhelming, but somehow she managed to turn the situation into a game and carefully pushed him away, again saying, with little conviction.

"Just behave yourself."

Somehow he did not seem to hear her, as again he pulled her towards him and this time she did little to resist him as he breathlessly whispered that he had forgotten how much he had missed her. He did not need to say how much, and it was obvious from his body language that he wanted her there and then as his hands caressed her back, his lips demanding kisses, and she felt his ever increasing firmness as he pressed against her. There was no need for words, as his natural observation skills were far ahead of hers as he gently took her hand and led her into her bedroom. She willingly followed. He adeptly pulled the curtains and turned to kiss her again, and at the same time began to take off her clothes, and asking her to take his off too. He flicked off his wristwatch and placed it on the dressing table.

They were both down to their underwear now, and taking a moment to breathe she glanced down to the enormous bulge in his shorts. At the same time he had taken off her bra and was teasing her nipples. She managed to bend down just enough to release him from his underpants and tantalising him, by gently, slowly touching him, as she did so.

'Ding Dong, Ding Dong' the front door bell rang out. Trying to speak through kissing his lips, she said she did not do cold calling and would not answer it. The bell sounded again, followed by a heavy thumping on her front door. Feeling very annoyed, she continued to say she would not answer the door, but the door bell continued to ring and the front door continually pounded. Neither Robert or she were able to concentrate, so she made a chink in the curtains and took a glimpse and she could not believe her eyes. There, parked outside her house was a police car.

Almost ignoring Robert, she opened the bedroom window and tried to sound calm, as she called down that she would be there straight away and without any explanation to Robert she asked him to get dressed immediately and to follow her down the stairs. As quickly as they could they dressed and ran down the stairs to the front door. She handed Robert his coat, and without any words, only a quick kiss, she opened her front door to let him out, and to let the policeman in. She was just able to glimpse a confused and agitated Robert drive off as she closed her front door.

Lindy showed the policeman into the sitting room, and at the same time asking him what on earth was wrong. Quickly a list of reasons he was in her house scrambled through her head; she had not had a car accident or perhaps someone had died and did not know her new address. The officer told her to sit down and to listen to him. The stern look on his face made her obey immediately, as she sat down, still confused.

He began by reminding her of her shoplifting arrest and then proceeded to say that the superstore were going to prosecute and she was due to go before a magistrates court in two week's time.

Lindy was speechless and began to tell him that she was innocent, but he put his hands up to stop her speaking, just like all the others, as he explained it was nothing to do with him, and all he had to do was to issue her with papers, and to inform her of what was eventually going to happen. Continuing to be unemotional he asked if she understood. She was only able to nod, as no words would come out as he then announced that he had finished his business with her.

She followed him to the front door, and just managed to say,

"Goodbye."

Closing the door quickly behind him, she turned around and was immediately sick in the hall. Her stomach wretched again and again, but she managed to contain the rest until she reached the toilet where she sank to her knees and vomited her heart out. When there was nothing else left, she lay on the toilet floor unable to find the strength to move.

Goodness knows how long she lay there, with her mind in overdrive as to what on earth was happening. The confusion went round and round in her head, as she lay there trying to make sense of her pending situation.

Later, having left the toilet she made a slice of dry toast, and nibbled at it as she struggled to find a way through. She watched the television, trying to distract her thoughts, but it did not blot out her buzzing, confused and depressed mind.

It was later in the afternoon that Tony rang to have a chat, and as usual to ask how she was. She was so relieved to hear him, but fought not to tell him about her sad and desperate situation. But Tony knew her well, and asked her what was wrong. Feeling at breaking point, it all came pouring out faster and faster, as she tried to tell him what had happened.

In his usual calm way he begged her to slow down and to tell him all over again. Having listened intently and without interrupting by asking questions, he suggested that a colleague of his would be able to help, and as it happened he lived fairly near to her. Tony said that he would put her case to him, and he was sure he would call her to discuss whether he would take on her case.

It all sounded very frightening but she thanked him and for his comforting words to her, and rang off.

Chapter Four

Lindy hoped that Robert would call with his suggestions for her painting; but, he was silent. After what had happened when they last met, she did not have the energy to contact him and knew it must have been a tremendous shock to him as well.

Alarm bells should have rung as Robert had not contacted her to ask what the policeman wanted or what was wrong, if anything or to enquire how she was. He just disappeared into his own private shell unable to cope. He was so obviously selfish and Lindy became increasingly aware of this dominant trait in Robert.

A couple of days later her telephone rang and as she answered it she hoped it would be Tony's friend who could possibly help her; thankfully it was.

He introduced himself as Malcolm and said that Tony had given him a skeleton idea of her situation and if he was to represent her he would have to ask her to attend his office the following day to discuss the whole situation in detail. Malcolm sounded very kind and with almost profuse thanks she agreed to meet him. He gave her his office address and politely said he looked forward to meeting her.

Thanks to her powerful car with its satnav, she manoeuvred her way to Malcolm's office. She did, in an isolated practical thought, wonder if the parking would be difficult but checking she was in the right place she parked and entered the building and was confronted by many brass plates of the firms working there. She did not know Malcolm's surname and was feeling very agitated but seeing a young woman she asked the way and was directed to the lift.

She knocked on the door and an immediate voice said,
"Enter."

This she did and came face to face with a rotund middle aged man with a very kind smile as she quickly introduced herself. He offered her a seat and something to drink. She took her seat but politely declined the refreshment, as there was no way she could even consider it.

Malcolm got straight down to business and asked her to start from the beginning. Lindy was prepared for this and started to recall her shoplifting experience with all the truth and accuracy she could manage. He listened closely to what she recalled and did not take his eyes from her.

He asked her directly if she had taken the ham and not paid for it, and immediately brought up the anger in her, as she explained that because of an operation several years previously she was unable to eat meat.

With this information Malcolm suggested she visit her doctor to ask for a written statement to prove that for genuine medical reasons she did not eat meat, and to ask for it to be sent to his office.

The meeting ended and he said he would be in touch before she had to appear in the magistrate's court as a preliminary necessity.

A week later Lindy was in the ante-room of the court. Malcolm was there to greet her and after asking how she was he continued without waiting for her reply. They sat down and he explained exactly what would happen. They would sit together and when her name was called she would be escorted to the witness box and the magistrate would ask her basic questions. He tried to comfort her as he said she would not have to say very much. Lindy nodded and sat very agitated as Malcolm made small talk while they waited.

Quite a while after the time her case was due to start he explained that sometimes business from the previous day overran and he was confident it was what was delaying them.

As the minutes ticked by Lindy found herself checking the clock on the wall and her wrist watch. Unable to ease her tension Malcolm said nothing until suddenly a voice in the hallway called her name and following Malcolm she entered the court. She had never seen one before and it was rather big. She was shown the bench seat as the clerk read out the details of her case. She was then asked to go to the box. As she did so she looked at Malcolm for confirmation. He smiled at her as she was told to sit down. Almost as soon as she did so her name reverberated in the room, and she was told to stand up and to look at the magistrate as she waited for him to speak.

She was asked her name, address and date of birth, and then the accusation was read out very slowly and very loudly.

She was accused of shop lifting and taking items without paying. How did she plead? Guilty or not guilty?

It took all her strength to reply in the calmest strongest voice she could find.

"Not guilty."

"You will be tried in court. Your representative will be given instructions as to when that date may be. Any failure to attend will result in your detention. You are dismissed."

Malcolm was there at the bottom of the steps and was smiling as he asked her to follow him into another small room. Lindy sat down because she would have fallen down otherwise, as she realised this was only the beginning. He explained the options she had before her, either to go to the magistrate's court again or the other option, to opt for a Crown Court.

He proceeded to explain that the magistrate's court would be as that day and they did see a lot of similar cases. The decision could go either way but that the crown court was a much bigger and more expensive situation but with a jury of twelve different people there was every chance she would be believed.

Overwhelmed by the experience she began to cry in fury as she shouted at Malcolm about her terrible situation and how unfair it all was and how untrue, but knowing she had to face up to it, and still wondering how it all happened in the first place. Her further thoughts made her almost hysterical with anger and frustration, and all her friend could do was to listen until she calmed down.

Having gained back some sort of dignity Lindy asked Malcolm what he thought she should do. His reply was,

"The choice of court is entirely up to you. If you can afford it I would perhaps suggest the Crown Court as there you will have the opinion of twelve unknown people."

Lindy exploded again and asked how on earth had such a situation got so out of hand, but after a long silence for consideration she said she would somehow find the money for the Crown Court and hire a barrister to plead her case. Malcolm sensibly suggested,

"If you do not have the funds then do not choose that option"

Lindy looked at him straight in the eyes and boldly stated,

"I will have the money."

He then confirmed that the next step was to get the doctor's report to clarify the situation before the Crown Court hearing and shaking his hand they went their separate ways.

Tony called sounding quite anxious and needed to know how her appearance in court had gone. Lindy felt drained but nevertheless alright and was glad to hear from him. She thanked him again for suggesting Malcolm as he was very long suffering, but the bottom line was that she was completely innocent and what Tony really wanted to know was that she had opted to go to the crown court.

With an audible intake of breath Tony voiced his concerns as to what a big ordeal that would be. She explained her reasons and he, almost begrudgingly, saw her point of view as he then went in to what she may have to go through and what to expect and added that the only thing he was certain of was that she was innocent and would be acquitted. Lindy thanked him for his confidence in her and excused herself from further conversation as she felt completely exhausted.

Lindy went to her computer to turn it off and saw an email from Robert. Having been silent since his last visit to her, she felt upset and irritated by his apparent lack of support for her as he had not contacted her to ask why the policeman was banging on her door, and had made no effort to contact her. She seriously felt let down by him, but she had to be true to herself and knew that it was not the first time.

Lindy opened his email with an almost bored approach to what he had to say and unfortunately she was not disappointed. He wrote that he would be interested in the painting her picture and added that he had another painting to finish and then after that he would contact her with his first basic sketches for her to consider. There was not a single word about anything else. Not even a kind enquiry as if she was alright.

Hurt and furious she turned off the computer without replying to him. One minute he is in a bad marriage and the next minute he is thinking of leaving it, then it was, 'We must be together', followed by silence. Followed by lust, then abandonment and now he was saying he wanted to paint her picture, which, perhaps with frequent bursts of sanity, she did not need.

She lay in the soothing hot bath as she kept going over in her head what a long a difficult day it had been and to finalise it she was so hurt by Robert's selfishness. They had been so close in the past, how could he be so incapable of making any kind gesture that did not involve his own best interests.

The bath towel was warm as she pulled it round her. She just had the energy to put on her nightdress and fall into bed and was asleep in seconds.

The sharp ringing of the telephone woke her up from the deepest sleep. It had rung several times before she realised exactly what was happening. She picked up the handset and managed a breathy,

"Hello."

It was Robert, but before she could even think of saying anything he was apologising for not being in contact before and wondered what was wrong when she had not answered his email. Still not speaking, but her mind was working fast as she thought that it had only been late yesterday that he had sent his email and what ... but before she could go any further he was asking if he could see her that morning to discuss the painting. Lindy explained that she was still in bed, to which he replied'

"In that case don't get up I'll be right over."

Trying very hard not to show her severe irritation at his brashness, she said that she would be pleased to see him in about an hour and he said he would call her just as he was about to leave. A flip! His thoughtful side seemed to be uppermost and she hoped it would last. Obviously satisfied at her reply he added in an enthusiastic tone the he was really looking forward to discussing the picture as the more he thought about it the more he wanted to paint it. Exactly what his alternative thought pattern was, she was not going to explore. She put down the phone and got out of bed.

During the time it took to shower and have breakfast her mood began to lighten as she started to think about how to make Robert laugh, to stop the negative thoughts she had towards him as a man. They always got on well when they were together and it was when they were apart, well mostly, that the tension began to mount. Her appreciation of the dramatic gave her an idea and once the idea took shape, she almost flew around the house to get everything in place. It was fun and exciting and by the time she had finished she fell back on to the sofa and giggled.

She wanted to put some music on but the phone rang and Robert said he was about a minute away. Trying to get the most out of her plan she said she would leave the front door unlocked so that he could come straight in without ringing the door bell, as she knew the chimes that hung from the curtain rail over the front door always announced when there was someone there.

Lindy sat and waited. In almost no time the set of three chimes tinkled and she heard his familiar voice saying,

"Hello."

She did not move, and did not answer, she only listened. He turned the key in the lock and then began to laugh. So far so good she thought as she listened to his laughter as he had obviously seen the small cut out sign of an arrow pointing upwards on the stairs. She stayed where she was as he called to her and she heard his footsteps as he began to climb the stairs to the sitting room.

As he reached the door he called to her again, but still she did not answer. The door was permanently propped open as she watched him peek into the room. His face beamed at her and he began to laugh again as he walked towards her, as she sat enclosed in a long cream coat that almost covered her, although her lower legs were just visible. She was wearing fishnet tights and very high heeled red shoes. She remained sitting down as there was no way she could walk in them.

Smiling in obvious appreciation he sat on the arm of the chair and began to ask her how she was as he started to gently pull away the high necked coat asking,

"What have you got under there?"

She just smiled and gently took his hand away, and then suggested he sit on the sofa so that they could discuss her painting and reminded him that he had said he would send her his base ideas but she had never received them. Barely altering his gaze he said that he had changed his mind and wanted to talk to her about them.

"Well! It would be nice if you had told me your change of mind wouldn't it?"

She looked deep into his face. She was not being harsh, just truthful, and it was obvious that he had not thought of that.

Robert got up from the sofa and again sat on the arm of the chair and with 'doe' eyes he said how sorry he was that they had misunderstood each other and as it was not very important then it was best forgotten. He bent down to kiss her saying,

"All forgotten?"

Lindy turned her cheek so that his lips did not meet hers. "I'm not sure," she managed to say as his closeness almost overwhelmed her.

She continued to sit there with the coat closed, still up to the neck as she again gently pushed his hands away as he tried to un-coat her, and insisted in knowing exactly what ideas he had for her painting. He went back to the sofa and slowly said,

"The lighting could be slightly more dramatic and perhaps an introduction of a horse pulling the feed for the sheep would be unusual but in keeping with the whole idea of the original canvas."

He got no further but walked over to sit on the arm of her chair and the same time bent down to kiss her. Their lips touched, but barely, as Lindy moved her head and managed to reply that his idea was really going to bring her picture to a new life, and added with great difficulty that the low lighting was essential as that was the key to her being drawn to the picture in the first place.

Robert kissed her cheek again and tried to open her coat. This time she allowed him to as she smiled and then began to giggle as she saw his face, as all she had on was an old t-shirt and an ordinary short dress. She just looked at him as he began to laugh. They laughed so much Lindy almost began to cry. Robert noticed her eyes welling up and asked what was the matter; his apparent concern made her feelings even more intense as she quickly brushed the tears aside knowing that were purely self pity as a reaction to her recent trauma and made a useless excuse by saying she was just glad to see him. It was a very lame excuse but it was right for the situation and his massive pride allowed him to accept it, whilst she had to silently admit that it was true.

Taking off her coat and with his warm hands in hers, he sat her down on the sofa right next to him and put his arms around her as she rested her head on his chest. She could hear the pounding of his heart and taking a big sigh she momentarily closed her eyes.

She did not move but opened her eyes, and all she could see was the hair on his chest as his chest went rhythmically up and down with each breath. Slowly she began to play with it and began to try and make patterns, and as she felt she was becoming quite inventive Robert moved and slid her arms around his neck and gently pulled her towards him, searching for her lips.

Caught up with the closeness of Robert she caressed his face, his head, his neck. He moaned to her,

"Don't stop."

She did not reply, she could not even if she had tried. The pleasure it gave her to touch him was extraordinary to say the least. He slid down on the sofa and Lindy felt his warm inviting arms gently pulling her even closer to him. His hands began to pull at her dress and then run up and down her thighs. Still kissing him, she opened her eyes and seeing him almost covered in the cushions which were over both his ears and part of his face she just broke away and started to laugh.

"What's so funny, Am I tickling you?"

"No," she replied still laughing, "I saw you almost disappear into the cushions and wondered if I would end up losing you and I hadn't even said a proper goodbye!"

At this Robert began to laugh at her crazy sense of humour as he lay there half propped up on the end of the sofa. As he studied her face he said kindly,

"You are the most bizarre woman I have ever met."

Trying to put on the pretence of seriousness she could only reply,

"This is musical comedy without the music," as she started to tickle him. He was very ticklish and she knew exactly where to touch him. Robert just dissolved into laughter and they hugged each other until they had both calmed down.

She went back to the real reason Robert was sitting so close to her which was the painting she had asked him to do.

"When will you be able to start?" she asked.

"Right now!" he said, and with a big grin put his arms around her and kissed her. Making a feeble attempt to stop him she tried to pull away but it was almost doomed to failure. It felt so right to be with him and she began to relax.

Suddenly she became almost limp and stopped kissing him and gently took his arms away, first one then the other. Not quite understanding he tried to embrace her but she slowly moved away from him and somehow managed to look at him saying in a quiet sad voice,

"You are married. You have said a few lovely things to me, but it looks as if you are leading me down the garden path with implications that your situation would change."

The look on Robert's face was one of shock mixed in with a flicker of embarrassment, but she could have been mistaken. Lindy got up and he did the same as she led the way down the stairs to the front door. He took his coat and just before he unlocked the front door, still not saying a word, Lindy felt a painful emptiness in her whole body; it almost engulfed her it was so strong, even though he was still there. She could not let Robert go without touching him again and so perching on tiptoe she kissed him on his cheek. As he went out of the door his silence was almost unbearable and all she could do now was to ask him to email his ideas for her painting. She clung to the door frame and watched him raise his hand in a wave as he drove away.

Chapter Five

Lindy's solicitor, Malcolm, called her to say that he had managed to get a barrister to represent her at the crown court admitting that he did not know him but he came with a very good reputation. He sounded very positive and explained that he had got him up to speed with her situation; adding that they would all meet in a side room an hour before her case was to be heard to give her a chance to meet her barrister and discuss the procedure.

When she put down the phone she felt it all sounded very intense but her reputation was at stake and she frequently puzzled as to what exactly had happened in the first place; but the fight for her innocence was paramount to her.

The day to day routine helped Lindy focus on her clients. She really enjoyed her work as a healer and counsellor, as she listened to their situations and feelings and helped whenever she could. Listening was the key and concentrating on her work took her mind away from her own problems.

Inevitably the day arrived when Lindy was due to appear at the Crown Court. Malcolm had arranged to pick her up from home, and so giving them time to talk and discuss the situation. As they drove along they chatted about this and that, and it was obvious that Malcolm was trying to relieve the tension, until he asked Lindy a question right out of the blue.

"Have you ever told anyone that you did steal from the supermarket?"

Lindy immediately felt as if her friend had become her enemy in a split second.

"Stop the car!" she shouted at him.

He took no notice and continued along the road and began to explain that it was a very pertinent question.

"I asked you to stop the car, please."

He did not reply, but found the next lay-by and pulled into it.

As soon as the car had stopped she released her seat belt and got out of the car and walked away. She heard Malcolm slam his door shut and his footsteps as they approached her. As he came nearer he explained that he had to ask her and added,

"I am sorry I have upset you but you must understand you may well get a lot of questions thrown at you today and you have to answer them."

"I felt you had turned on me and didn't believe me," she said feeling slightly less angry.

"Please get back into the car because if we meet any hold ups on the road we could be late and that is going to look bad, especially as your barrister will be waiting for you and that will certainly not give him the right impression."

Feeling a little more confident they got back into his car. There were no traffic delays and they arrived only a few minutes late, and hurrying along the corridors they reached the room where Lindy was to meet her legal representative.

The formalities soon over, she looked at him and knew she had to trust him even though they had only met a few minutes ago. He was tall and in his mid-forties and possibly had dark hair, but under his grey wig it was difficult to be certain. He had an air of superiority about him and soon dominated the situation, and speaking slowly and clearly, but hardly taking a breath he outlined his understanding of her case.

In what seemed like next to no time at all their case was called. As difficult as it was Lindy had to ask to go to the ladies' room before she went in, and even had to ask the way. She relieved herself as quickly as she could and went back in to the corridor where Malcolm and her barrister stood waiting for her as they ushered her in to the courtroom. She was shown where to sit and the two men took their place in front of the bench and she noticed next to them was another barrister, a woman.

The jury was then selected as one by one different men and woman were asked if they knew the accused and also if she objected to them, for whatever reason. They were a variety of ages and of both sexes, which, when she had a moment to think, she thought was probably a good thing. Once selected they were all sitting on the jury benches, and almost immediately the clerk of the court told everyone to stand as the judge entered the courtroom. He then announced in a very loud voice the case that he had before him.

The prosecution called for the store detective to go to the witness box. It was then that Lindy saw the woman who had accused her of stealing. She watched very carefully as she stood and took the oath on the Bible. Then the questions started as the woman was asked to recall the day in question that she accused Lindy of shop lifting. Having outlined her story she was then asked how long she had been in her job.

"Two years," came back the confident reply.

Then she was asked if Lindy had offered to pay for the goods.

"No," came back her reply.

Almost beside herself with rage Lindy said in a loud whisper to Malcolm.

"It's not true!"

He turned frowning at her and put his fingers to his lips to silence her.

Shortly afterwards the store detective was asked to step down.

Next it was her barrister who got up and began with a statement from her doctor who had in very complicated medical jargon explained that due to her medical history Lindy was a vegetarian. Before all this she had no idea what her doctor had said and felt so glad that he had explained it so explicitly, although it was not good that her personal details were shouted out for all to hear, but at least it was true.

Her name was called as she had agreed to being questioned. She stood in the wooden box and took the oath.

The woman prosecutor asked if she had money problems. Then she was asked if she was buying food for a friend. Then did she have any bouts of memory loss. And all that Lindy could reply was,

"No." " No." And again, "No."

The last question came from her barrister,

"Did you offer to pay for the item even though you knew you did not want it?"

"Yes, I did offer to pay," she replied relieved to have the chance to tell the truth.

"That is all my Lord," her barrister said, and she left the box and went back to her seat. The judge left and the jury filed out.

Malcolm suggested that they have a light lunch in a good café he knew just down the road. He assured her that his mobile was now turned on and as soon as the jury had reached a verdict he would be informed. Grateful for the fresh air they walked the short distance to the café.

Drinking her lemonade and munching her fish salad made her feel much better although at first she did not think she could eat a single morsel. Malcolm had a coffee and a large steak and chips, and she watched him as he enjoyed every mouthful. Anxious to finish the meal before being called back to court he was eating quite quickly and so they ate in almost since.

They managed to finish their meal and walked slowly back to the courthouse, but there was still no word from the jury, so they took a seat and waited patiently. As the time ticked by Malcolm began to fidget and turned to Lindy and almost unable to keep looking at her he began to say that he was beginning to have some concerns as normally such a case would be decided in a short time. But trying to be positive he added that perhaps they were taking a long lunch break. His kind attempt to humour her did not sound convincing as they sat and waited and waited. Then suddenly there was a flurry of movement that indicated the jury was coming back followed by the Judge.. As they took their places Lindy watched them as they sat down one by one. She did not know what to do as she scanned their faces but they did not look at her.

The elected speaker stood up and was asked if they had reached a verdict and he replied,

"No, we cannot agree."

"Can you reach a majority verdict?"

"No, my Lord we cannot."

He did not look at Lindy as he sat back down again.

The judge ruled that the jury were dismissed and ordered a re-trial to take place within the next few weeks, and everyone got up and left.

Malcolm admitted that he was stunned by a hung jury although he did wonder what was happening when so much time had gone by with such a short case. He vowed that her re-trial would completely exonerate her.

They drove back in almost silence and declined a cup of tea and said he would be in touch very soon, and drove away.

After pouring a glass of wine and drinking half of it straight down she called Tony as she had promised to tell him what had happened. When he picked up the phone all she could say was,

"They could not agree. I have to do this all again quite soon."

His sharp intake of breath and kind words to her were just too much as she suddenly burst into tears. Poor Tony, his kindness to her had brought on a sort of self pity. Lindy was well aware that anyone being genuinely caring towards her threw her into an emotional turmoil. Grabbing a large tissue she tried to stem the flow of tears as they streamed down her face, as she tried to speak to Tony. His continued supportive words did not actually help her regain her composure, but he stayed on the line.

Still dabbing at her eyes and nose Lindy started to speak to Tony and was able to thank him for his unswerving support. Realising that she devastated and exhausted he suggested that he could again mix business with pleasure and admitted that he had 'put to one side' the drive to one of his ongoing clients, but if they could meet up and have a laugh it would make it more bearable for them both. He added, almost as an aside, that they could go out and take dramatic photographs of the wonderful countryside where she now lived.

As long as it did not pour with rain she said it would be a wonderful idea. She again thanked him for his support and belief in her and said how much she would look forward to seeing him again, camera in hand.

He laughed and said,

"When I can book a hotel to coincide with my client I'll let you know, and I'll check the weather forecast and hope that the forecasters are right!"

In the past when Tony had been on work in the area he had visited her and they had tried to explore some areas of outstanding beauty and those that were steeped in history. Lindy had heard about Malham Cove and had suggested they go there to see for themselves, and grateful for the diversion from his work Tony readily agreed.

He arrived cheerfully on the doorstep on a day when it was a bit misty, with a forecast that the sun would melt the early mist away, so undeterred they left with cameras on board. It would be quite a long drive but they had lots to talk about and catch up on, so the miles just flew by. The visibility was still poor but they were sure that the promised sun would soon shine through.

As they got nearer their destination the roads became quite narrow and the few cars approaching them had their head lights on, but still feeing optimistic Tony drove on. The road signs indicated that they were almost at the Cove but the mist was even thicker now, almost fog as they continued and discussed their options. If Malham was so big, surely they would be able to at least see it even if the light was not good for photography. Tony kept driving until they had missed a turning. Confused, he slowed down and they discussed their next move, whilst continuing to climb up through roads with snow covered fields on each side. Suddenly the fog lifted and the weak sun shone through. They stopped and looked at the breathtaking scene that was before them; the lovely high hills and the miles of fields separated by the wonderful dry stone walls that went on to almost eternity. Lindy had always wondered how on this earth such an amazing feat had ever been completed so long ago as there were almost no hedges to divide the fields one from another.

As they looked at the sight a couple of keen walkers came striding passed the car and Tony asked for directions to the Cove. They pointed back to the direction they had just driven through.

Looking back they could see the obvious line of fog with the sunshine they had found, so, turning the car around they descended into the fog, but soon they both agreed it was not the day to see the Cove and decided to drive back stopping off at a small country pub for a delicious lunch.

On his next visit Tony suggested they have another go at finding the elusive Malham Cove. Lindy agreed it was a very good idea as they had been so frustrated at their first failed attempt. Fortunately the day was dry and windy and the white clouds scudding across a clear blue sky gave them confidence that there would be no fog that day.

Once again they had loads to talk about and as they turned off the main road on to the country roads Lindy was able to admire the wonderful scenery; they even came across a board inviting people to try dry stone walling. She was tempted but they had other plans that day.

Then they rounded a bend and there, right in front of them was the dramatic cove in all its glory. It was enormous. Although they were about a mile away they felt as they were driving straight into it.

Tony had to stop the car as he burst out laughing and each accused each other of being stupid not to have noticed such an amazingly large historical sight that they had so easily missed on their trip before.

"How could we have missed this before?"

Tony asked in between his bouts of laughter, and all Lindy could reply was

"What do you mean by missed; do you mean mist?"

They arrived, parked the car and walked the short distance to the base of the rock.

It was a very good day for photographs as they happily clicked away.

Mission accomplished.

Chapter Six

Lindy was always pleased to see Tony as although his visits were short, they were almost always action packed.

She was grateful for her work too and had been recommended by a couple of her regular clients to their friends so her life was quite busy. Sometimes they visited her at home and other times she visited them in their homes; the latter was preferable to her as she could then see their environment which gave her a deeper understanding of their personality.

She always checked her emails and phone messages so that she did not miss anyone who may request her help; in its several forms.

There had been none from Robert and it had been a few weeks now since he had left her in silence. She was disappointed but not surprised as she had been outspoken before, but this time it seemed she had made a very good job of pushing him away. But she knew it was not what she wanted at all, as she recalled how happy, open and vulnerable she was when they were together and was always aware of tingling all over. No one had ever made her feel so totally alive and vibrant. Their sense of humour was very similar too and he somehow always brought out in her the impish ideas that made him laugh. On more than one occasion he had just flopped down on her sofa in almost complete disbelief at her 'madness' as he obviously struggled with her unpredictability. The look in his shining eyes was enough for Lindy to know he appreciated her plans and she could see he was able to forget the outside world and the pressures that it brought, if only for a little while.

Their respect and mutual appreciation of each other was wonderful, and would have been the envy of all their peers, if they had known about it!

But they did not know her secret of the passionate, private and highly charged relationship which was so difficult to hide, for both of them.

Perhaps, she reflected, Robert had found it too overwhelming when she had told him the truth as he wasn't always very good with basic facts when they were thrown at him. He was a gentle man and Lindy knew she had been too harsh, even if it was true. It was his almost innocent streak that had attracted her to him in the beginning, apart from all the other assets he possessed which complimented hers.

Malcolm rang to say that the next court hearing was in three week's time and insisted she would be cleared completely. Lindy thanked him and breathing a sigh of relief that at least she knew the plans, she put down the phone.

Almost straight away it rang again, and she picked up the receiver expecting it to be Malcolm having forgotten something. There was a short silence and then Robert's voice came into her ear. His tone was straight and businesslike as he apologised for the delay in getting back to her with his ideas and asked when it would be convenient to visit and show them to her. The surprise call took her off guard as her emotions welled up in her and she only just managed to control her voice as she checked her diary and suggested a couple of dates later in the week. Robert said the following day would be a good idea, and with a notable softening in his voice he seductively, almost whispered, that he looked forward to seeing her again. It was not what he said, more how he said it and their call ended.

There it was again; the pull towards him and she sat down again feeling a bit confused. Lindy had waited for his call expecting that it would be soon after they last met, but it never came. There had been several times since then when she had regretted even asking his opinion on her idea for him to paint in his own inimitable style. This time she vowed things would be different, as she began to think that maybe it would be best if whatever he suggested, she would say that it just did not enhance the original painting. She remembered having had similar thoughts before to discourage him in the past and once again this emotional tug of war was happening as she fought with the real knowledge that their relationship was too complicated. Another thing she acknowledged was that he could easily email his ideas to her, which would give her a chance to consider them. They had actually talked about this in the past and Robert had always said everything can be done by email these days!

Lindy went to her computer and carefully wrote an email to Robert, suggesting he email his ideas and added that she was grateful for his time and looked forward to receiving them. She read and re-read her letter to him and holding the 'mouse' the cursor went to send, and as she pressed it the front door bell rang, making her jump. As she had been so intent on her idea it took a moment to realize what was happening as she walked to the front door and opened it to a client holding a bunch of wild flowers. As soon as she saw Lindy she smiled and said she was glad to find her in and the flowers were to say thank you for all the help she had been given. Lindy invited her in but her client insisted she had another appointment and with a cheery smile waved goodbye. Grasping the flowers she went back in to the kitchen, and as she arranged the beautiful flowers she reflected that simplicity almost always wins over exotic as she placed them on her window sill; then she returned to her computer to see if there had been any reply from Robert.

There wasn't a reply, well! It hadn't been that long since she had sent it. Feeling uncertain she went in to her 'Sent' box and there was nothing there. Feeling frustrated and slightly irritated she searched to find the -mail she had sent to Robert. There was no trace that she could find and as time was going on, she had to either compose another one or accept that he would visit her the following day. Her head buzzed round trying to balance one thought against the other and eventually she decided that she would not be a coward and looked forward to seeing Robert. She quietly scolded herself for being so indecisive, and had to admit reluctantly, that she did want to see him again. The good the bad and the seriously cheeky was how she put her situation with him.

Shortly after 10 a.m. her house phone rang. It was Robert and said that he would be with her in about five minutes, and asked,

"Shall I ring the bell or come straight in?"

She had chimes over the door which alerted her to anyone coming through the front door, should she have forgotten to turn the key in the lock.

"Come straight in, drive carefully."

She unlocked the door and went into the kitchen to put the kettle on to offer him a drink; that was the least she could do and only polite to any guest, and placed two cups on a tray with a couple of biscuits. She had only just sat down when the familiar door chimes rung and his unique voice called out,

"Hello I'm here."

She heard him turn the key in the lock, and without saying a word, she listened as he climbed the stairs to the sitting room. She had left the door open and soon his face appeared looking slightly uncertain. Getting up and without touching him she just said,

"Hello, would you like some tea or coffee?"

"Tea please," he replied.

"I know, with one sugar too."

He stood right next to her and she could hear him breathing and felt his breath on her face, but she fought the almost overwhelming desire to touch him and hug him. All she managed to do was to deflect her feelings and invite him to sit down and make himself comfortable and get ready to show her his ideas for her painting whilst she made the tea.

She spilt his tea in the saucer the first time around so had to start again. How ridiculous, she said to herself, he's only a man and how many cups of tea have I made over the years? She put the cup in the sink and got out another set, saying to herself, just get a grip, but holding on to the side of the worktop was not the answer.

She panted and puffed before taking the tray to Robert, whom she found lounging back on her sofa. He did not move, only said how peaceful it was and gently smiled at her, as she handed him his tea and offered a chocolate biscuit, which he accepted. She then sat down beside him, and listened as he crunched. There was a few minutes silence as Lindy tried to look at the artistic ideas he had to show her. She could see that Robert knew she was keen to see his drawings, and it seemed that he very slowly sipped at his tea, as he generally asked after her work as they chatted together each getting an update on their lifestyles.

Robert lifted his cup high to take the last dregs of tea and then carefully placed it back in the saucer.

"That was very nice, thank you, I usually drink from a pot."

That meant a mug to Lindy, but she did not query his words, as there were many sayings and northern rituals she had yet to learn.

As he opened his folder he patted the side of the sofa and invited her to sit close to him so she could see exactly what he had planned for his interpretation of the 'Twilight' painting. She moved slightly closer to him as he opened up the folder and took out sketches of his ideas. She knew she must not touch him, and fortunately she was able to look at them and still keep a small distance between them. After a minute or two she could feel the warmth radiating on to her skin, and asked him to pass the sketches to her. Intent on his work, he did so and she focused on his ideas.

Whether by calculation, mistake or providence as he passed the last paper to her their hands touched. It was as strong as an electric shock, as it fizzled its way through the whole of her body and finally rested around her heart. As her pulse raced as she was aware of Robert looking at her with his hands in his lap; but their bodies were now touching each other as they sat there side by side. Apparently concerned that Lindy had not replied, Robert moved slightly so that he leaned towards her and at the same time pressed closer to her. Still trying very hard to concentrate, Lindy looked at the sketches through blurred eyes as she saw less and less, becoming increasingly aware of Robert sitting beside her and his warm body against hers. She continued to look but the page was just a blur, and as her heart began to race she heard his gentle voice in her ear simply asking if she liked them. Like it, she thought, is he mad, like it? Of course I like it. Like his sketches or like his nearness to her? Struggling to keep a level tone to her voice she just managed to breathily say,

"I like it very much, please will you paint it for me?"

She knew that Robert had been looking intently for her answer, as he then smoothly turned to her and after a fleeting glimpse at her face he slowly leant over to kiss her, pecked his lips on hers and drew back just enough to see if she was alright about it, and then kissed her again, this time with more confidence As Lindy's hold on Robert did not give way their lips met and their mouths opened and she tasted his chocolate lips. They enjoyed each other, and not wanting him to stop she made a sort of soft moaning noise, still kissing him. At this he broke away,

"What do you want?" he asked, almost innocently.

Lindy began to slowly pull away, realizing it would not be the right thing to continue, considering his circumstances.

Still gently holding him she looked straight into his shining questioning eyes, as she admitted to him,

"I want to enjoy what you obviously want and offer me, but your unchanged situation is far from right, and I find it very difficult not to respond to your advances because you know how I am attracted to you but I really struggle with your situation.

As she spoke to him she released her touch on him, and with immediate sadness in his eyes he started to straighten his clothing. With an obvious effort he said he had to leave, and looked forward to the final decision of his ideas on the painting.

She followed close behind him as he descended the stairs to the front door in silence, but halfway down the stairs Robert suddenly turned around, knowing she was close behind him. Feeling his genitals about to burst, he urgently unzipped his trousers and flipped up her skirt. Lindy, just for a ,aw his engorged penis but too late as he spread his seed all over her.

They lay together on the stairs until Robert recovered himself from his uncontrolled release, and all Lindy could do was wait in silence for him to explain himself. After what seemed like ages he moved to kiss her and with no apology at all continued down the stairs. She watched as he let himself out of the front door and still lying on the stairs she heard him start his car engine and then drive away.

She felt the tears well up in her and still partly lying on the stairs she felt a deep sadness creep over her that made her cry and cry; this was not how it should be.

Chapter Seven

It was the day of her Crown Court hearing, and Lindy struggled to know what to wear, feeling both optimistic and depressed all at the same time.

True to his word Malcolm arrived to pick her up for the drive to the courthouse. The roads were busy as they got caught up in the business commute to work. Road works added to the congestion which made Lindy agitated, but Malcolm took advantage of the delay to go over the details once again. Lindy knew he was trying to be helpful but looking at her watch and being stuck in traffic she found it very difficult to concentrate on what he was saying. She tried to be helpful and polite, but after only a short time she asked him to stop asking questions and to please get to the court on time. Realizing she was in a state Malcolm apologised and in silence he negotiated the traffic as best he could.

Time ticked on and they were still some distance from the court and Lindy could not help but say that they were going to be late, as they had to park as well. She looked at him and saw his mouth tighten, but he said nothing. The traffic seemed to ease and Malcolm was able to pick up speed and they finally arrived at the time of their hearing. Malcolm offered to drop her off outside the main door but feeling in need of his support she said she wanted to be with him as they entered the court. Fortunately as it was fairly early in the day there were quite a few empty spaces, and Malcolm parked his car easily and together they ran into the court building. The clerk was obviously waiting for them as they breathlessly told him the case. He smiled and speaking incredibly slowly he said that the case from the previous day had overrun and they had time to compose themselves. Together they sat down to catch their breath as she wondered how people doing the job of clerk to the court managed to be so unemotional. It had to be a gift, and she knew she had not been given it! Seeing the water cooler she got up and asked Malcolm if he wanted some cold water. He said he did so she took two plastic cups and with her hands still shaking, she passed one to him. They sat together sipping the refreshing water as Malcolm went over a few details again.

An hour went by and they still had not been called. The water had gone through now and she found her way to the 'Ladies'. Standing at the sink washing her hands, she glanced in to the mirror. Oh dear! What a sight reflected back at her, she saw a pale face devoid of the usual colour with great black bags under eyes, and deep lines etched everywhere; she looked like a wild animal and almost did not recognise her reflection. She took out her comb and carefully flicked her hair trying to give it more body as it clung close to her head, with no bounce at all. That was a major sign of stress, she thought as she tried to alter her looks and she certainly did not like what she saw.

A loud banging on the toilet door and Malcolm calling her immediately brought her back to the moment and grabbing her handbag she almost flew out of the door.

"Our case it next," he said.

They entered the large intimidating room and Lindy was ushered to 'the box' with a strong grip on her elbow from the duty officer. They remained standing until the judge entered, soon followed by the members of the jury, as they approached one by one. She was instructed to look at them and agree they did not know each other and that also Lindy had to agree the suitability of each one of them 'trying' her.

The formalities over, her case began.

The prosecution solicitor rose and stated the crime against her and then called the store detective to give her evidence. It had only been a few weeks between the court appearances but Lindy thought the woman looked different this time, but eager to hear what she had to say she concentrated on what lies she had to tell! This time she seemed to falter a bit but perhaps, Lindy thought, it could have been her imagination or just plain wishful thinking. Then one question was asked.

"Did the accused offer to pay for the stolen goods?"

The answer was short and clear.

"No."

At that stage Lindy's fury took an immediate hold on her and she called to Malcolm who was sitting just below her in his professional seat.

"That is a complete lie." she said in a stage whisper.

Malcolm looked at her and put his fingers to his mouth to stop her talking anymore. Almost possessed with frustration she sat and watched her reputation being destroyed.

The store detective had finished the questions from her solicitor and then it was time for her barrister to rise and ask her his queries. As he stood up the judge intervened and congratulated him on becoming a Q C. He bowed very politely and said,

"Thank you m'Lord."

He turned to the woman in the witness box and asked if her recollection of the events were true. She visibly took a deep breath and said,

"Yes it is."

He let a few seconds pass, still looking at her, he then asked,

"What position have you in the store today?"

"I work on the tills," she feebly replied.

"I'm sorry I did not quite hear what you said, would you mind repeating it?"

"I work on the tills."

Her voice was much stronger this time, as the colour visibly drained from her face.

"You work on the tills now do you?" He turned to address the jury and he calmly stated, "I have no further questions."

Next it was Lindy's time to take the stand as she was ushered in to the witness box and gave her oath to tell the truth. The date and time were presented to her again as the prosecution tried to unhinge her, with, 'Had she taken the goods?' 'Had she not paid for them?' All her answers were a defiant,

"No"

But the other question was missing, and he did not ask her and sat down.

Lindy's barrister rose and looking straight at her asked,

"Have you told the truth today?"

"Yes," was her breathy reply,

Suddenly she felt emotional and almost started to cry in frustration. Seeing her obvious distress her barrister began to ask the court's permission for a short recess, but Lindy came back from the brink and managed to say,

"Thank you I am alright."

"Did you offer to pay for the goods that it is alleged you took?"

"Yes I did, when I was in the manager's office."

"Thank you, that will be all."

She wanted him to ask so many more questions but he sat down and she was ushered from the box.

"That concludes this case. Will the jury please retire to consider your verdict."

Lindy stood up as the judge left and the jury filed out. Not one of them looked at her, as she almost fell back on to her seat. That was it now and she knew she could do no more other than to wait. Malcolm came to help her down onto the level court room floor, as he enthusiastically said that he thought the whole case had gone very well. She just managed a polite,

"Thank you very much for all you have done."

The waiting game began. She did wonder where her barrister had gone and Malcolm said he had a special room where he could wait and probably work on his other cases, and added that even he was not allowed in there!

After about half an hour there was movement in the court and Malcolm confirmed it seemed that the jury was coming back in. When everyone was in their place the judge asked the foremen of the jury if they had reached a verdict.

"Yes, my Lord," was his clear reply.

"What is the verdict of you all?"

"Not guilty, my Lord."

"Is this the conclusion of you all?"

"Yes my Lord," came back his strong voice.

The judge turned to Lindy, who was almost unable to move and said, without smiling,

"This case should never have come to court. You are dismissed."

Lindy made a slight bow to him as he left the courtroom, closely followed by the jury. She watched them leave and wanted to say thank you, but only one lady quickly glanced at her, but had no expression on her face.

As the last person left she leant heavily back on the bench as Malcolm almost flew up the stairs to congratulate her, but all she could say then was,

"Oh God, I just wish I didn't need to ever go shopping again."

Feeling slightly light headed she asked for a glass of water as she knew her legs would not work until she had recovered her composure.

During the drive back home and beginning to feel a bit stronger, she asked Malcolm how this all occurred in the first place?

In some of her darkest times she had wondered if the meat had been planted in her trolley, and if so, by whom and why? It had never made any sense at all. On her better days she had wondered if someone had mistaken her trolley for theirs, but as she had hold of it for most of the time it did not answer any of the questions to her satisfaction.

Malcolm reassured her that she was completely acquitted of the so called offence and that in six weeks her records would be destroyed and she would have a clean record, and rightly so. Lindy had not thought about that side of things and it was obviously of the most ultimate importance or, again in her deepest darkest times she thought she may be struck off the professional register and would be unable to work again.

As they arrived at her front door she invited Malcolm in, but he politely declined and admitted he was very tired and needed to get home and if possible do some work for the following day. He enthusiastically shook her hand and smiled as he said she would receive his bill and the barristers in the post in the next few days. Lindy thanked him again and got out of his car and waved as he drove away. That was another thing; she had not had the opportunity to thank her barrister for his extraordinary appearance, but she would add a note when she paid his bill.

Chapter Eight

Having had the last few months dominated by the court cases, Lindy found it difficult to get back into her normal routine. She had been optimistic that she could still see her clients but to her frustration, she knew she could not do them justice and had cancelled them and re-booked wherever possible. Instead, she visited her friends and getting drawn in to their lives helped her to heal. Some knew of her trauma but quite a few did not. Just to be able to put it behind her was paramount. Even Robert did not know, but she had always thought it was nothing to do with him. This was true especially as he had never asked about the policeman's visit when he was there, which really upset her. Their closeness had never allowed for personal downtime, although she had often listened to his worries.

She had not had any contact with Robert since he left her on the stairs in an distressed and emotional turmoil, and knew she had to decide how she wanted her painting to develop; that was the next decision she had to make, not only because she wanted to see the present painting on her wall transformed into how she had grown to perceive it, but to also be able to look at it every day and see something different, and to feel drawn into the scene and be part of it and to sense deep admiration and emotion of its basic natural beauty. As far as she was concerned Robert was the only artist who was able to satisfy her idea, but, and there was a but as far as she was concerned, he had to soften his edges; she needed him to mellow his painting lines.

With all this in mind she totally concentrated her mind on his ideas he had given her the last time they met. As she recalled the day, she felt her emotions rise from deep inside her, as she scrutinized his work, and just seeing his thoughts made her feel alive as his emotions transferred to her eyes, and into her. She languished and wanted to tell him what she was going through as she longed for his support and his closeness.

Lindy examined Robert's ideas and then left them on the floor of the room and closed the door. She needed to think and feel without seeing, so she drove to the nearby riverside, parked and slowly walked along the bank. It was a pleasant bright day as the sun peeked out from behind the clouds from time to time. The weather encouraged dog walkers and she smiled as they passed by. Deep in her thoughts she was almost run over by a cyclist who rang his bell loudly and as she had not heard him it made her heart jump. She stood still on the narrow grassy verge that she had to retreat to that led down to the river and watched the current take along leaves and small twigs as they bobbed along. There were lots of ducks that appeared out of the long grasses breaking their camouflage in the hope for food as they smoothly paddled towards her, which made her wish she had thought to bring along some bread, but all she could do was to say,

"Sorry ducks."

There were a couple of majestic swans too that looked at her but did not swim over. A short distance ahead was a fallen tree whose branches dipped into the river, alongside the sturdy weeping willows, and their reflection on the water when the sun came out was clear and naturally beautiful. She noticed a broken down wall on the other side of the path, so she stepped across the footpath and carefully negotiating where she sat she semi perched on it to take in the whole scene and to feel natures soothing atmosphere bathe over her.

The reason Lindy was there had not left her thoughts as she recalled the original painting had a small insignificant stream on one side, and to emphasize too much movement would distract from the main theme. She knew that balance had to be just right and to take it down into a gully and with slight movement portrayed would perhaps give just the depth it needed. Thinking about the gully unexpectedly brought back the memories of Ethel her dear friend from the hotel, when they went for their walk in the dewy grass and feeling positive, she got up and slowly walked back to her car trying to think which one of Robert's ideas was the right one. She knew what she wanted, but how to get it? She would have to look at his ideas that she had left abandoned on her sitting room floor

As she entered her front door she realized that the fresh air had made her hungry, so after taking off her jacket she went straight into the kitchen, opened up the cupboard door and took out a tin of soup. That should do the trick, she thought as the aroma of the warming meal drifted into her nostrils, and as soon as it was ready she spooned it into her mouth, being careful not to scald her lips. Then the phone rang, so putting down her spoon she walked to answer it. The client on the other end, with obvious restraint, asked if she could have an appointment. Caught slightly unaware she hesitated for a moment, but feeling positive, invited the client to see her in a couple of hours. This agreed the grateful client rang off. The temperature of the soup was just right now so she enjoyed every mouthful. She wanted to look at Robert's ideas, but had to quickly collect up his work as she had to prepare the room and herself for her client.

The appointment with her client took slightly longer than usual but Lindy felt it had been beneficial. She tidied up the room and with the CD of healing music still softly playing she sat quietly for a few minutes and studied the painting she was so fond of. The walk by the river had helped a lot so she got out his sketches again and remembered that it was up to her now to contact him if she liked any of his ideas, or perhaps it would sensibly stay unaltered as Lindy was only too well aware of the increasing complications of their intense relationship.

Whilst still deep in thought and trying to make a decision the phone rang which made her jump. Very much to her surprise it was Robert, his voice sounding soft and slightly hesitant as he politely asked if it was convenient to talk for a few moments. Feeling a sudden surge of emotion she felt her heart begin to race as she concentrated on sounding in control. It was a complete lie and she knew it, but she had to at least try.

"I have just seen a client and have a few moments."

That sounded a bit rude so she quickly added,

"I have been contemplating your ideas for the painting."

"Oh good," he replied, his voice sounding more confident now.

"Have you decided yet?"

Again the thread of uncertainty crept into his voice. As she pressed the phone close to her ear she could just hear him breathing.

"Yes Robert I think that I have; perhaps a combination of your sketches and an idea I had only early this morning."

"That sounds very interesting. Are you going to tell me what it is or email it or if you are not too busy, perhaps I can bob in and see you?"

It was a lovely local phrase and with his soft sensual voice in her ear and his obvious enthusiasm to see her, Lindy had only a second to decide. Almost without any conscious thought going through her mind she heard herself making arrangements for him to visit shortly.

Lindy was in the kitchen when the front door bell chimed; taking a deep breath she walked to the front door and opened it to the beaming face of Robert. He closed the door behind him and turned the key to lock it. The dangling chimes were still tinkling as he turned to face her and with no words spoken they blended into each others' arms. Feeling him touch her made her slightly skittish and she leant away from him but still with her arms tightly around him.

"Are you going to let me put my keys down and take off my jacket?"

"No," was her impish reply as she only slightly reduced her hold only to tighten it again. Laughingly they hugged each other as she let him go. He did not take off his shoes, as is the northern custom, as he followed her into the kitchen for a cup of tea. While the kettle was boiling they stood with their arms around each other talking un-recallable nonsense.

Tea made they went to the sitting room where they sat down on the sofa side by side. Lindy tried very hard to turn the reason for his visit to the sketches which were again on the floor on the mat in front of the fire, just under the original canvas under serious discussion. She heard him suck in the tea, perhaps to stop him from scalding his mouth, but she dared not look at him for fear of catching his eye. She had heard that some people still poured tea from the cup into the saucer to cool it down and then tipping it slightly slurped it from the side as she briefly imagined him doing that. It was barely a second but she began to giggle. Although they were not touching each other Robert sensed her mood and asked if she was alright?

Trying very hard to push her mental image of him slurping tea away she struggled to keep a straight face as somehow the sound was still in her head, but she turned to him and seeing his kind quizzical face so close to hers she faltered before quickly gathering her thoughts together and simply said that she was glad to see him. He was not drinking his tea from the saucer but smiled broadly and moved as if to kiss her. Sensing it, she turned as his lips softly touched her cheek. The input of such a simple act had a big reaction within her as she fought to keep some sort of composure. Still feeling the warmth of his body radiating towards her she managed to ask Robert which one of his sketches he liked the best to fulfil her idea of the new painting of an old one. He glanced at the one hanging on the wall and then down to his idea. He was silent for a few moments. She broke the silence by telling him about her walk along the tow path that morning and the idea that had come to her.

Robert glanced at her silently, acknowledging that he had heard, and then looked at the work spread out in front of him. Lindy relaxed back on the sofa and watched him as she saw him concentrate his mind for the challenge that she had set for him. Little had she realized the complexity of the task when she had innocently asked him for his help.

During the continued silence Lindy began to question the need for the painting as it could be interpreted as merely a whim. She remained sitting back and in the corner of his eyes she caught a glimpse of a smile; it was not his mouth but in the corners of his eyes as they began to crease only slightly as he sat artistically composing his professional opinion. The vibes between them seemed to go back and forth without a single word being spoken, and apart from his breathing he sat completely still. It was times like these that she felt at one with him and she treasured every second.

Robert shifted slightly and at the same time let out a long sigh as he turned to speak to her, apologised for taking so long and added that he knew it was important to her and needed to concentrate. He went on to explain that he had not quite decided how to start and that so often he was presented with a blank canvas and always felt that the key to a successful painting was the initial composition.

During the time that Lindy was watching Robert she had thought about the copyright laws which she was well aware of because of her interest in photography. She knew that any reproduction of any artistic work without the consent of the original artist was against the law, so she put her concern to Robert who assured her that in this instance it did not apply, and accepting his superior knowledge they started to discuss their 'masterpiece'.

He picked up his teacup to drain the last dregs out of it and shuddered as they were now cold. Lindy immediately offered to make him another one but he declined and said looking straight in to her eyes,

"I don't need hot tea to make me feel the way I do when I am so close to you."

Keeping her gaze he moved and put his arms around her and slowly brushed his lips on hers. It was so smooth and gentle and so inviting. As he slightly released his hold he again looked at her. Seeing the uncertainty in his eyes she did not know how to respond as he took her face in his hands and again brushed his warm lips on hers, this time seductively taking a little longer. She had been here before and in a fleeting second had to decide how to respond, but before she had time to do anything he had deftly swung her legs over his at the same time lifting up her skirt to expose her knees and she watched as he stroked her legs and gently kissed each of them, almost in homage.

This swift movement had left her almost lying on her sofa and she witnessed a scene as if it were almost not her own as she watched an intangible, slightly purple cloud rise above him and then embrace them both only to disappear as quickly as it had appeared.

It was the awareness of his body that could not be ignored as she felt the warmth and increasing firmness of his erection as it began to grow, so she moved, only slightly so that he could have more space as it almost felt as if he would break out of his trousers.

"What do you want?" was her pathetic question.

"To see your stockings and to look at your beautiful smooth skin," was his soft reply.

Using every single ounce of her now weak self control Lindy gently lowered her skirt and carefully took his hands and put them on his knees, and trying to ease the situation she could only smile and say,

" Please, just behave. Perhaps I have been wrong in asking you to paint this picture for me? You know how I appreciate the style of your work and that is why I asked you. We both know we have a strong bond together, but I do not appreciate being taken advantage of, and that unfortunately is how I feel."

Her tone was straight as she looked at him and waited for his reply. She watched, his expectations dashed as he sank into the opposite corner of the sofa. He raised his head and with his big shining eyes looked deep into her as she felt his passion, although he was not touching her, only scanning her all over.

Struggling to find any remnants of composure she felt his magnetic pull on her and tried to avert her gaze. He said nothing as he continued to look at her with inexorable desire but a second later his phone rang. As he picked it up from the coffee table he rose and walked away as he answered it, and she watched as he controlled his voice and then walked out of sight into the hallway. When he returned it was a different face she saw as he explained it was one of his important clients who needed information, and said he had told them he was out but would call as soon as he got back to his studio.

He quickly gathered up his possessions and with a warm kiss on her lips he opened the door to let himself out at the same time saying,

"I'll be in touch very soon."

The days went by but Lindy knew it was not over, far from it! There was so much unfinished business between them and their history together was increasing with every situation that happened between them. She was, although reluctantly, getting used to big gaps between the times they met, and not having quite finished the final details of the 'masterpiece' left her frustrated. Fortunately she was quite busy with her clients and only hoped that when Robert called again she would be free to see him, and decided that fate was in charge, again!

Having had a leisurely breakfast and reading a magazine Lindy felt relaxed as it was the first day that she did not have any appointments. The radio was playing gentle music in the background as she put her dishes into the washer, pressed the controls to start the short cycle and went upstairs to shower and wash her hair. The warm water was soothing and the shampoo always smelt good as she lathered it on to her head. Then she thought there was a sound and reduced the flow of water to listen more carefully, and yes, it was her telephone. She quickly grabbed her towel and dripping wet stepped out of the shower hoping that the caller would not hang up; she could have let her answer machine click in but felt compelled to answer the call and with wet hands she lifted the receiver up to her soaking wet hair and said,

"Hello."

"Hello." It was the familiar voice of Robert. "Have I caught you at an inconvenient time?" he asked.

"Well sort of," she truthfully replied, "I was in the shower and I am dripping all over the carpet"

"I'll keep it short then. Can I come and see you this morning, so we can finish our plans for your painting? Would around eleven be time enough for you to dry off?" His voice broke off in to a cheeky laugh.

"I don't know, what time is it?" she replied. "But I am sure I can be presentable by then, but you may find a carpet firm here drying out my house," and she began to giggle too.

"I'll take my chances and will inflate my water wings just in case you need to be rescued"

And before she could find a snappy retort he rang off.

Smiling and giggling out loud she stepped back into the shower and quickly finished off her bathing as she realized she only had about half an hour to look half decent and be calm enough to receive Robert. She could feel the excitement of seeing him again gradually welling up inside her and took several deep breaths to try and stop the feelings overwhelming her, as she flicked through her wardrobe trying to find something suitable to wear, having to admit she wanted to please him. Finally with little time to spare she chose a comfortable light violet blouse and a three quarters length skirt, as it gave out the sign of femininity whilst still private. She slipped into a pair of black high heeled shoes and noticed her red hair was glistening as she checked herself out in the mirror before going downstairs into the sitting room and nervously started to pump up the cushions.

Her door bell chimed and her heart began to race uncontrollably, so taking more deep breaths she slowly walked to the front door and opened it to a smiling Robert carrying a bunch of flowers. He stepped in to the hall and with a serious face said,

"These are for you and I am so sorry that I had to leave so suddenly last time we met."

"Thank you they are lovely," she just managed to say breathily,

"I'll just put them in some water and arrange them later."

He slipped off his jacket and hung it on the baluster and was soon right behind her as she went in to the kitchen.

"Where are they, have they been or are they coming?" Robert asked, referring in jest to the non-existent carpet men, at the same time putting his arms around her waist as he leant against her and kissed the back of her neck, which sent a quiver of goose pimples all over her. Unable to do anything as her hands were occupied, she could only giggle which made him do it again as he continued to gently press against her so that she could feel his arousal. All she managed to do was to wiggle a bit which allowed her to turn around as she teasingly flicked some water at him and as she turned she noticed that he was wearing exactly the same violet coloured shirt as her blouse, and being so struck by the co-incidence she had to mention it.

"Great minds think alike," she said

"Fools seldom differ," was his immediate reply with a grin.

She explained that spiritually it is recognition of like minded people who, although apart, are both thinking similar thoughts, and colour is a visual confirmation of their oneness; the colour is similar to the crystal stone Amethyst, which is considered to be seductive and a sign of friendship, but a very intriguing and complex gemstone. He laughed as they walked to the sitting room.

They both sat down on the sofa and in mock sternness she suggested they get to the point of why he was there. As he had caught her by surprise earlier she had forgotten to put out the sketches he had previously made and just as she realized she stood up explaining she would go and get them. He immediately assured her that it did not matter, as he had given the 'Masterpiece' some considerable thought during his absence. He sat quite still and concentrated on the painting as Lindy watched his face, until he turned to her.

"I think it is a blessing that we did not decide earlier as all I think is necessary is to add some muted light in the windows of the house for added warmth, and to define the church in the distance to make everything more lifelike, as if you could imagine walking along the winding road to wherever it leads, or wherever the sheep are going to."

And cleverly added,

"Usually it is sheep that follow on, but this time it is the observer who follows the sheep. What do you think Lindy? I think there were too many alterations last time which would have altered the atmosphere it already radiates."

Lindy studied the painting as he spoke and realized that he was completely right and smiled at him saying,

"I knew you were the only one to change it and make it right. Thank you so much."

Robert quizzically puckered up his lips, inviting her to kiss him. Unable to ignore him she gave him a peck on his pursed lips as they both started to laugh and with barely a noticeable movement they were in each other's arms and sensuously kissing, as the subtle change from art to physical attraction was effortless and natural as she responded to his eager mouth on hers. He caressed her and whispered as she became unable to resist his attention and his obvious increasing desire; they slid down the sofa in a passionate embrace. Lindy still tried to slow him down with the odd word or two as she released her lips from his but he just smoothly and carefully came back to kiss her lips with his teasing tongue, as again she knew she could not resist his advances and now she did not want to.

His sexual power over her was magnetic as she responded by running her hands over him and just managing to artificially complain that he still had all his clothes on and with an audible sigh of mock boredom he released his hold and undid the top buttons of her blouse and asked her to undo his shirt. As she did so she ruffled his hair and it was so 'cute' that she had difficulty not to say so as he was kissing her again, when suddenly her house 'phone rang and made them both jump

"It's alright, I'll let it ring," she said breathlessly. But it kept on ringing and her answer machine did not click in and somehow she knew she had to answer it. She was glad she did as it was a client who desperately needed her help and opinion of a very difficult family situation.

The call had broken the intense situation between herself and Robert and just by looking at his face she knew how sad he was as she explained as best she could, without breaking client confidentiality, that she had been aware of the situation and had to try and sort it out and had to leave straight away. She sat down beside him and hugged him, wanting him close to her but knowing she had to leave. Fortunately Robert understood her situation and did not try to keep her from her work and as he composed himself he took her hand in his and together they walked to the front door to say goodbye for the time being. They hugged each other again and Robert let himself out saying he would call her the following day as they had so much unresolved work to be done as reluctantly she let him go.

There was no time to dwell on the situation with Robert as she had to review her clients' notes before setting off to meet them, and as she was refreshing her mind she found herself distracted, which was unusual for her, becoming acutely aware that she needed time to consider her own future and hoped there would be enough time for quiet meditation before Robert's call.

As so many times in the past, Robert did not call and as the hours went by, in spite of being busy, Lindy's thoughts turned to her own feelings and knew that they ranged from a caring understanding of hopes and plans to anger and frustration and an ever growing recognition that she really needed to know what she wanted and at what cost to her emotionally. This unenviable position she found herself in, raised conscious acute questions that had to be addressed as they kept flying through her mind.

What did she really feel for Robert? And perhaps more to the point, what did he want from her long term, if that was going to be a possibility. If only there was someone in her life that she could count on and talk to and with whom she could feel confident that they would understand her situation, with a guarantee that they were mature enough to make a valuable contribution and have an unquestionable opinion. Both her parents had died young but they had never been close anyway, so there was only one person left - herself. Lindy knew she had to rely on her own feelings and desires, with an enormous amount of plain old fashioned common sense.

As she tried to settle her mind down she smiled to herself 'common sense?' Well that seemed to have gone out of the window and she wondered when it had begun to take a backseat, and her internal conversation replied; it had been the first time she had spoken to Robert.

Chapter Nine

It was two days later that her house phone rang; it was Robert, his voice as always let her know immediately how he felt. This time it was firm but also apologetic as he quickly explained that he had been through a difficult time at home and with an almost pleading voice ...

"Please may I visit you today? I can leave straight away, if that is convenient and I can tell you all about it."

Trying to sound calm and casual and with her heart pounding in her chest she agreed, adding that she was looking forward to seeing him, and with trembling hands she replaced the receiver. As luck would have it, or fate, and now she was confused which was which, Lindy did not have any clients booked in. As she cleared the kitchen table she looked down and could visibly see her thundering heart beating at a tremendous rate and turned off her radio. She checked that the rooms were moderately tidy and at the same time thinking what a rollercoaster of emotion and passion they shared and wondered if their soulmate relationship, that was so vibrant and alive, made other nice but ordinary liaisons mundane and routine?

It was a short time later that the now familiar tinkling of her chimes over her door so beautifully announced Robert's arrival. He cheerfully called out her name at the same time as she emerged from the kitchen to greet him, his shining eyes and smiling face always plucked at her heart strings as they both walked towards each other and without a word were in a loving warm embrace. There was no need for words as they clung to each other. Lindy could feel his tension gradually melt away as he gave out a big long sigh, and slowly released his arms enough to softly kiss her lips and slightly pulled back to scan her face before he kissed her again.

Hand in hand they walked into the sitting room and sat down side by side. Still nothing was said as again Robert let out another sigh as he relaxed back on the sofa; and all the time Lindy was watching him and wondering exactly what had happened to him and what had he to tell her. She gently stroked his tense hunched shoulders and as she did so she felt the pent up tension in him slowly drain away.

Lindy waited for him to speak first as it was obvious there was so much he had to say when suddenly he turned to her and blurted out,

"I have left her. After all this time I have left her, I just could not go on living a lie. It was all so sudden. I just looked at her across the table as she explained in minute detail what she had to do to prepare the meal for us and how I did not compliment her on every aspect of her hard work. She just appeared like a machine to me so I had to get up without saying a word and made a call to a good mate of mine who I know has a big house and asked if I could stay the night.

"Fortunately, being a bloke, he did not ask any questions and said it would be fine. I packed a small bag and left without saying where I was going, and now that I have had a moment to think about it she did not follow me or ask where I was going, as she knew what I was doing. I expect she thought, he will be back soon to finish this lovely meal I have cooked! I wanted a break up but I never thought it would be like this. I know it is completely the right thing to do but I did not expect to feel so bad, and I know I want to be with you. I love you Lindy."

Lindy's eyes filled with tears as she watched the man she loved unburden his feelings to her, and in spite of his emotional trauma she found the strength to ask him if he wanted to go back to the life he had just left and added that now was the time to make one of the biggest decisions of his life; to either return and try to do the right thing or to follow his heart which was obviously with her.

Robert was not a harsh man, it was not in his nature and as she continued to stroke his shoulders she could see the pain in his eyes as he came to acknowledge the crossroads in his life.

Realizing that they needed total privacy Lindy gently released her hands off him and leaned over to turn his mobile phone off and then walked over to her telephone and pulled out the plug. No-one and nothing was going to interfere this time. She knew that Robert was aware of what was she was doing but did nothing to resist and as she sat down beside him they melted in to each other's arms and hugged each other.

Lindy kept her arms around him until he gently moved his head to kiss her with his gentle sensuous lips. He kissed her again as he swung her legs over his thighs and stroked and caressed her as his kisses became more intense and inviting. He moved only slightly and took both her hands in his and carefully pulled her to stand up, as again he pressed himself to her and took her hand to guide her to feel his intense arousal. There was never a second thought as she had always felt the need to follow an overwhelming power that seemed to take over control when they were together! And he certainly had a beautiful contour and he felt so good, she thought, trying with absolutely no success to be strong enough to resist him. He guided her up the stairs and quickly removed his trousers to allow for his erection to be free. He undid her blouse and unhooked her bra, quickly taking them off as his hands played with her as she stroked, enjoyed and appreciated his body.

Together they fell on the bed and as he lay there looking at her he pulled her on to him and cupped her breasts in his hands, when suddenly she said,

"You have got your hands full there haven't you?"

"That's what they were made for," he said as they both started to giggle. But his kisses were too much and his hands were everywhere as he reached down to touch her, to feel her wetness and in a second he was in her as he gasped out with emotion. They moved slowly together at first not wanting their heightened sensation to end but it was all it needed for them to find the ultimate climax between them as they both cried out in their final release.

They stayed together, locked in the wonderful sensation of satisfaction and as they lay there Lindy could not help herself as she gently ran her hands up and down his back as his breathing became more regular and deep. He had totally relaxed and had fallen asleep.

It was only a haunting sound of a train horn in the distance that disturbed him. He kissed her and rolled over,

"You went off then," she teasingly said.

"I should say I did," he replied and she was unsure as to whether he had understood her, but it didn't matter as they were completely happy together.

There was only a short while to be intimate together before Robert was in the bathroom under the shower. Lindy leapt up to pass a big white fluffy bath towel to him so that he would feel comfortable. He called out through the sound of the shower to say that he was expected back at his friend's house for an evening meal and could not be rude enough to be late as he was so grateful to him and his wife for taking him in at such short notice and they had not fired questions at him as to why he needed shelter.

He dressed, as Lindy put on her dressing gown to go down the stairs and say goodbye. They held hands as Robert turned to her and with a straight face said,

"I don't know how this will work out as there are a lot of things to sort out but I will see you tomorrow to tell you the plans as they are progressing."

"You can always live here," Lindy said breathlessly.

"I know," he replied. "But it is not as simple as that at the moment. I have to legally get what is due to me and to learn how a separation unfolds."

He kissed her once more and unlocked the door.

"It is for the best, the best for everyone," he said convincingly as he walked out of the door and down the driveway to his car. He waved and smiled as he drove away.

Chapter Ten

As she slowly closed the door and turned the key to lock it, Lindy was all too aware of the potential changes about to have a serious imminent impact on her life.

If anyone could have planned the perfect relationship it was certainly not her and Robert's, but the undeniable and overwhelming need and desire to be together was what 'fate' had for them, and 'she' is a very hard task master.

Lindy slowly climbed the stairs and walked in to her bedroom where the subtle scent of his aftershave hung welcomingly in the air. She had not been aware of it before when he had been with her but it enveloped her thoughts as she perched on the edge of the double bed where they had made love so beautifully only a short while ago.

She undressed and slowly walked to the bathroom still thinking of him. After all the tumultuous emotions of the past there were now possibly serious and solid promises of a happy and fulfilling life to look forward to as she ran a deep bath and watched it as it rose up almost to the top. Then her sensible side took over as she thought, 'I must leave enough room for my body so as not to overflow on to the floor', and poured in essences of lavender, camomile, lemon and jasmine just before she turned off the taps and swirled it around to be absorbed in to the inviting warm water.

As she relaxed, all the years of struggle to find true inner happiness gradually melted away as she vulnerably lay in the bath and played. As her sponge sucked in the water she squeezed it over her head and felt the water drip on her face and flow down as the droplets splashed back into the bath. Tears welled up she inhaled the whole sensuous feeling and aroma and gradually slipped under the water to feel the softness that would help her to release the emotional traumas she had endured for almost as long as she could remember.

The warmth was comforting, gentle and all embracing as she settled down on the bottom. She imagined a peaceful life where everyone was happy and momentarily she saw Robert in the water too and together they swam to meet each other and blended into each other in an osmotic life, forever to be together. Then her breath ran out!

The thought of being with him drew her towards the most beautiful love and there was no going back.

She had held out her hand to him and her heart was resting in it. He had so carefully taken it and together they had made love.

They had made a vow that, if ever either of them could find their tears in the ocean then their spiritual love would dissolve, but they had made the promise to each other knowing it was 'earthly' impossible and so they were bound together for ever; and would probably live happily just off the M7!

Lindy laughed at her own nonsense, and softly began to hum to herself feeling her heart would burst as it seemed like a lifetime of sadness had been washed away, and finally she felt completely whole as she slowly began to sing ...

> For all we know we may never meet again,
> Before you go, make this moment sweet again.
> We won't say goodnight until the last minute,
> I'll hold out my hand and my heart will be in it.
> For all we know this may be only a dream,
> We come and go like a ripple on a stream,
> So love me tonight, tomorrow is made for some,
> Tomorrow may never come, for all we know.

Her emotions were high and she was truly happy.
She felt a whole person at long last.
Now she could sing without the tears falling.

True love is a wonderful gift
Embrace it with all your heart.

For All We Know

Words by Sam Lewis
Music by Fred J. Coots